A DOUBLE

Aileen Armitage

severn
House

This title first published in Great Britain 2001 by
SEVERN HOUSE PUBLISHERS LTD of
9–15 High Street, Sutton, Surrey SM1 1DF.
Originally published in 1975 in Great Britain under the
title *Empress to The Eagle* and pseudonym of *Aileen Quigley*.
This title first published in the USA 2002 by
SEVERN HOUSE PUBLISHERS INC of
595 Madison Avenue, New York, N.Y. 10022.

British Library Cataloguing in Publication Data

Armitage, Aileen, 1930-
  A double sacrifice
  1. Napoleon, I, Emperor of the French, 1769-1821
  2. Love stories
  I. Title
  823.9'14 [F]

  ISBN 0-7278-5786-X

For David

Except where actual historical events and characters are being
described for the storyline of this novel, all situations in this
publication are fictitious and any resemblance to living persons
is purely coincidental.

Printed and bound in Great Britain by
MPG Books Ltd., Bodmin, Cornwall.

CHAPTER ONE

PALACE OF SCHÖNBRUNN, VIENNA: 1800

'DON'T just hurt him, Louise; *kill* him!'

Terror stared from the little boy's blue eyes, blenching his thin cheeks and causing him to wring his bony hands in agitation as he pleaded with his sister. By the light of the candles which blazed in thin gilded sconces he could see her solemn face framed by golden curls as she bent pensively over the moulded wax figure in her hands.

'It won't do, Ferdinand, I can't get it right. Let us search out your ugliest toy soldier and we'll use him instead,' she replied thoughtfully at last. Ferdinand rushed to the huge toy cupboard obediently and began ransacking it, throwing aside balls and dolls in feverish haste. Louise watched silently, her blue eyes glittering.

'Make haste, Ferdinand, or your governess will return before we are done,' she urged. Ferdinand pounced on the box of soldiers and thrust it into his sister's hands. Louise was so cool and capable, a big girl of nearly nine while he was only six. She would know what to do.

From the lacquered box she selected a soldier carefully. 'This one will pass," she murmured. 'He is ugly and his paint is flaking off. He will be perfect for the Corsican beast.'

Ferdinand shuddered, as he did whenever that monster was mentioned. From babyhood he had been terrified of the name of Napoleon Bonaparte, the upstart from Corsica who, from obscure beginnings, had risen swiftly and insidiously to become the most terrifying creature in Christendom. Even Aja, his governess, paled when she spoke of him and occasionally had recourse to threaten the wilful Ferdinand with the bogeyman. A ruthless creature, she said, who as rumour reported ate naughty little children for his breakfast.

'So do as you are bid at once, child, or he will come here and gobble you up,' she would admonish. Ferdinand's inordinate fear of the Corsican brute was shared by all his younger brothers and sisters, even Louise, the eldest. Not even the Emperor's children could escape the fear of Bonaparte that haunted the heart of every Austrian child.

Louise drew a long bodkin from her pocket. Ferdinand watched in horrified fascination as she lifted the toy soldier from the polished table, her eyes glittering anew with hatred.

'Will it work, Louise? Will stabbing the doll really hurt—him?' Even now, with Napoleon Bonaparte lying vulnerable in Louise's delicate hand he could not bring himself to say that fearful name. Louise nodded.

'My Aja, Madame Colloredo, swears it is witchcraft and highly effective if one hates sufficiently. You do hate him, don't you Ferdinand?'

The boy shivered and nodded convulsively.

'And so do I.' Louise raised the bodkin. 'May he suffer and die in agony!' she cried, and brought down the sharp point viciously. Ferdinand gasped as the needle penetrated the doll's stomach but did not quite pass through it. Louise stared at the mutilated doll and suddenly the room, though warmed by a huge log fire, seemed to grow chill and menacing from the atmosphere of fear and hatred that they themselves had engendered. Ferdinand began to cry.

'I'm frightened, Louise!' His trembling lip and agitated white face stirred his sister's compassion, and laying aside the doll and bodkin she enfolded him lovingly in her arms.

'There is nothing to fear, silly. It is but a doll and cannot harm us.' But from her dilated blue eyes Ferdinand could see she too was afraid, afraid both of the monster Napoleon himself and of the terrible thing they were doing in the secrecy of the nursery, the plan born of abject terror, to kill the Corsican ogre by witchcraft, if they could.

'But what if he discovers what we have done, Louise? What will he do to us? We have only hurt him, not killed him, haven't we? If he finds out, he may come marching into Schönbrunn and do something terrible to us.' Ferdinand began whining plaintively. Louise snatched up the bodkin again.

'Then we must be certain we have destroyed him, Ferdinand, and all will be well.'

Horror-stricken pale eyes watched Louise's arm rising and plunging again and again, stabbing venomously till the bodkin pierced the tiny figure utterly. 'Hate! Hate!' she cried shrilly.

'Hate! Hate!' echoed Ferdinand, though less certainly, fear quivering in his voice. To his distraught mind the very shadows in the corners of the vast chamber seemed to close in menacingly upon them, returning wave upon wave of the hate-filled emanations that proceeded from him and Louise. He clutched her arm imploringly.

'No more, Louise! Stop it, please!'

Louise stared at the bodkin, broken in her hand. She looked up sharply at the sound of rustling which came from the direction of the tapestry screen which stood near the high double doors of the nursery. Ferdinand watched, mesmerized, for the spectre of Napoleon Bonaparte to appear, wrathful and bent on revenge.

But it was Madame Colloredo who advanced briskly into the room. In the absence of his own adored aja, Ferdinand flung himself gratefully into her reassuring skirts. Louise's aja patted him comfortingly.

'Come now, children, what is amiss?' she demanded brightly, then wagged an admonishing finger at Louise. 'I have been seeking you everywhere, Your Highness, to help you prepare for dinner. It is not fitting for an Archduchess to be unpunctual, and your papa the Emperor would be most disappointed in you if you were to appear late at the table.'

'I am sorry, Aja. I was playing with Ferdinand.'

'And what game were you playing?' Aja's sharp eyes were regarding the mutilated doll on the table.

Ferdinand looked up fearfully. 'We were killing the Ogre,' he whispered, barely able to confess the enormity of their crime.

'That is good,' Madame Colloredo pronounced. 'All patriotic Austrians hate the Corsican upstart and swear to bring about his downfall. That is a good game. Come now, Marie Louise, or we shall be late.'

As Marie Louise was leaving, Ferdinand's aja appeared at that moment and bore him away. Madame Colloredo seemed highly pleased by the game she had inadvertently chanced upon in the nursery, reminding her charge as she brushed her long silken tresses of their victim's heinous crimes in the past.

'Such a creature, Your Highness, so greedy and wicked! No honest, God-fearing creature is safe from his predatory clutches, not even kings and emperors. Why, even your own dear Papa has suffered from his avarice! The Ogre likes nothing better than to march with his dreadful army upon some innocent monarch, stealing his land and destroying, snatching his crown and palaces and murdering his people.'

Marie Louise listened patiently. She had heard it all

before and especially from Madame Colloredo whose hatred of the Corsican was as fierce and fervent as her love for her young mistress.

'See how pale and harassed your dear Mama looks, fearful of the Ogre's next foul action. And your Papa too, always alert and apprehensive for the safety of his family.' Madame's tongue clicked sorrowfully as she tugged at a stubborn tangle of curls, and Marie Louise winced.

It was true, Mama looked always pale and fragile, even distant and reluctant to be comforted by Marie Louise's eager embrace. 'Don't fuss me, child. Your fingers are sticky and I do not feel well,' she would say. The ethereally lovely Maria Theresa, second wife to the Emperor Francis, was perpetually occupied with bearing yet another royal babe for the royal nursery. Aja, seeing the child's disappointment, would offer her loving arms instead, and Marie Louise had long ago learned to accept Madame Colloredo as the mother-figure who listened and loved and sympathized as a mother should.

Aja was the head of Marie Louise's vast household, for as a royal Archduchess the child had acquired her own Kammer at the age of two. Two ladies of the bedchamber, two ladies of the wardrobe, a lackey, a master of the furs, a washerwoman, a head nurse, a footman and a hairdresser hovered constantly within call in her own suite of apartments in Schönbrunn Palace. Thus, invisibly yet undeniably, was the royal child, eldest of an ever-increasing brood, barred from the intimacy of family life while Mama Colloredo grew in importance to her.

There had been other ajas before Madame. There had been the Countess von Wrbna, then the Countess Chanclos, both of whom she had loved dearly until her mother saw fit to replace them, but none so well-loved as Mama

Colloredo was now. For she was not only a very great friend of Mama the Empress, but she also had a daughter—Victoire, who was the same age as Marie Louise and her dearest friend. Now, with Aja and Victoire to love, and all the babies in the nursery to caress and fondle, life was indeed contented. And Marie Louise's greatest love of all, the joy of her life, was her proud and handsome Papa.

Mama was charming and gracious, true, but Papa was clever and gentle and made no secret of his adoration of his little Louise. Like her, he was openly demonstrative of his feelings with those he loved and shy with strangers.

'You are so like your Papa, Marie Louise, it is uncanny,' Aja would say approvingly.

'Am I like him, Aja? Am I really?' the child would exclaim in pleasure.

'In personality, yes, though perhaps more like your mother in feature.' There was no denying the pendulous lower lip of the child's trustful mouth, the mark of all the Hapsburgs. The fullness smoothed out into a wide smile of contentment.

The sound of the dinner gong reverberated along the endless red-carpeted corridors of Schönbrunn Palace. Accompanied by Aja, Marie Louise made her way down to the great dining hall in pleasant anticipation. For once she was to dine in state with her parents instead of alone in her Kammer as was usual. For once Papa was home from his endless State progresses and visits to foreign monarchs and reviews of his armies, and for once Marie Louise could revel in the sight of him and bask in his loving approbation.

But tonight Papa seemed preoccupied. He did question Aja as to Marie Louise's progress before the royal family seated themselves at table, and nodded absently in reply to Aja's assurances that Her Highness worked diligently at her studies and was as obedient, truthful and submissive as any parent could wish. Marie Louise was quick to perceive her father's air of abstraction, and wondered why it should pain her far more than her mother's obvious indifference.

'Come, let us begin,' said the Empress, her tone of boredom dismissing Aja, who curtseyed low before leaving, and recalling the Emperor's attention. Francis smiled apologetically. 'Forgive me, my dear, for I have much on my mind. My intelligence from the army varies by the hour, and I know not whether Italy can repel Bonaparte or is being crushed by him. I expect news from Marengo soon.'

Marie Louise bent her attention to the delicious food placed before them on golden platters, knowing better than to intrude her unsolicited conversation upon her parents. Etiquette was strict and inviolable in the Austrian Court. Marie Louise tucked into the braised beef contentedly, ladling over it huge quantities of horseradish sauce. The empress watched distastefully, not touching her own plate.

'Louise, you Naschkatzerl!' she exclaimed. 'Must you gobble all before you like some starving urchin from the streets?' Marie Louise sat meekly, eyes downcast.

Francis arched his eyebrows in surprise at his wife's outburst, then remembered her condition he patted her hand which lay, languid, on the damask tablecover.

'Do not reproach her, my dear. She has but a healthy child's appetite, as she has always had. We should be grateful we have such a healthy daughter.'

Maria Theresa sighed and leaned back in her gilded chair. Unceremoniously the double doors crashed open and a military envoy, still cloaked and mud-spattered, stood white-faced and hovering uncertainly. The Empress scowled angrily. Emperor Francis, seeing the look of agitation on the man's face, dropped his napkin to the floor as he rose to meet him.

'What news, man? What news from Marengo?'

'I have ridden non-stop, Sire. I am faint.'

'Bring wine!' Francis cried, and Marie Louise could see the fear dilating her father's eyes while the man drank thirstily, his bloodshot eyes red as the wine within the cup.

'Lost, Sire. Marengo is lost, and Italy is fallen,' the man croaked at last. Francis sank weakly into a chair, and the Empress moaned softly before she swooned. Servants came scurrying to attend to her, bearing her away to her apartments, but Francis still sat, stunned and silent. Marie Louise and the travel-stained envoy both sat uncertainly, the one sadly awaiting his master's next orders, and the other, unaware of the terrible import of his news, deciding to carry on eating alone.

Mama Colloredo was quick to point out the significance of this latest event to her charge. 'This monster Napoleon Bonaparte is invincible, it seems, and your poor Papa fears for his own life and yours. If only someone could find the means to destroy that wicked beast! All night His Imperial Majesty and my husband the Count have worked and discussed the problem, but they are no nearer a solution, I fear.'

Stricken as the little Archduchess was with pity for her father's plight and fear of the Ogre's coming here to destroy their peace, she soon forgot the problem when Aja brought Victoire to play with her. Studies over, the two girls could escape the choking discipline of the court and rush out to play in the secluded alleys of the gardens, far from the Empress's reproachful gaze. Victoire was such a joy to the dutiful little Archduchess with her bright eyes and lively mind, inventing all kinds of novel games and daring escapades which sometimes made Marie Louise gaze at her in loving awe. And even if Mama did not really approve of her friendship with a mere governess's daughter, Aja herself obviously did, her often frosty features sunlit as she watched them at play.

But Mama would not permit Victoire to visit too often, and between her visits Marie Louise's time was passed in boring studies of French, in which she was not over-talented, and Latin and Czech and Hungarian and Italian—and music, which she adored.

'You are lucky,' little Ferdinand growled to her one day. 'I have to study all those things *and* history and politics. You and Leopoldine and Caroline don't, you lucky creatures.'

'That's because we're girls. You are the Crown Prince and one day you'll be Emperor like Papa, and you'll need to be clever,' Marie Louise retorted, but kindly. 'Especially,' she added as an afterthought, 'if you mean to overcome foreign rulers who are wicked, like Bonaparte.'

She thought little of the Corsican tyrant these days for, the attempt at witchcraft failing to harm him, she managed to forget him except on the occasions she was obliged to remember his existence. As, for example, when the beloved grandmother whom she had never seen, Queen Marie Caroline of Sicily, left her home in Naples to come to Vienna.

'Are you to stay with us on a long visit?' Marie Louise demanded joyfully. Her grandmother smiled thinly.

'A very long visit, my precious. I fear that peasant upstart, Bonaparte, has robbed me of my Kingdom. Now I have no home unless you will have me here.'

'With pleasure, grandmama,' Marie Louise exclaimed, and after being mentally cross with the Corsican beast for his greed in stealing yet more palaces from Europe's royalty, she promptly forgot him again.

Life continued in its usual routine way for the little Archduchess. Few changes occurred in the austere daily routine except for the arrival periodically of a new royal baby in the nursery, another pet to cuddle and caress. Mama remained distant and dictatorial and Papa warm and loving—when he was home, which was seldom. Aja and Herr Kotzeluch, her tutor, filled the child's time monotonously, and the only ripples of pure pleasure came from secret, earnest confidences with Victoire in a secluded corner, or best of all, a mumured conversation alone and a loving caress with Papa.

His deep voice, vibrant with love, sent shivers of unalloyed happiness through his adoring daughter. Without doubt, she repeated often to herself in the stillness of the night, her father was the dearest creature in the whole world to her. For him she would walk through fire or flood, or brave the very terrors of Hell itself, and never pause to question.

CHAPTER 2

VIENNA, 1805

THROUGHOUT the next few years in Marie Louise's life, a constant discipline of implicit obedience and submission enlivened only by her love of music and flowers and her collection of pets, the spectre of Napoleon Bonaparte appeared and receded frequently. Word came to her shocked ears of the Monster's defeat in Egypt at the hands of the intrepid English sailor, Nelson, and of the Beast's humiliating flight. Austrian hearts rejoiced, but the little Archduchess was scandalized by Bonaparte's treachery, leaving his soldiers betrayed and effecting his escape only by denying his faith and pretending to be a Mohammedan! It was sacrilege!

Aja made sure her charge came to hear of all the Corsican did.

'Now he has declared himself First Consul of France,' she told the wide-eyed eleven-year-old. 'Before long he will aim higher.'

And at twelve Marie Louise heard how the murderous brute had assassinated the Duc d'Enghien, son of the Prince de Condé. A Bourbon prince, shot by Napoleon's order, was the Ogre's way to clear his own path to the throne, Aja explained. And very swiftly Napoleon proved her surmise correct, for he declared France an Empire and then had the audacity to have the Pope himself come to Paris to crown the upstart Emperor.

Next he declared himself King of Italy, and in place of

shocked surprise in Vienna, a new atmosphere of unease began to pervade the air. Even Marie Louise, until now pre-occupied with the diversions of having Victoire to take tea and poppy-seed rolls in her Kammer and even to sleep with her overnight, forgot the delights of her pet-house and personal garden when she saw Aja's blanched face.

'What is it, Mama Colloredo? What makes you so pale?'

'I fear for us all, my child. They say the French army is on the road towards Austria. Even now my husband the Count and your father are deep in debate in the Emperor's study.'

Marie Louise could visualise them, solemn-faced and urgent, her father seated in his richly-carved chair before an inlaid desk, maps outspread before him.

'What will they do, Aja?' The princess's voice trembled with apprehension. Madame Colloredo folded her into her arms.

'Fear not, sweetheart. The Count urges the Emperor to accept the Tsar of Russia's invitation to join him and England and Prussia in an alliance against the Monster. Between them they will be strong enough to defeat him. We shall be safe yet, God willing.'

Marie Louise crossed herself. 'Please God you are right, Aja.'

It was Victoire who informed Marie Louise that evening that her father had succeeded in persuading the Emperor to join the alliance. 'And now it seems your Papa is to invade Bavaria, the Ogre's ally. Is he not brave?'

'Indeed,' the young Archduchess replied gladly. 'My father is brave and good and kind, and I am proud of him. He will rid us of the Monster, I know, for he is wise as well as courageous.'

And trustingly she fell asleep in her wide canopied bed with a night light burning comfortingly nearby and Aja within call in an adjoining chamber. Strange, but for all the Palace's vast colonnaded beauty Marie Louise infinitely preferred the family's summer residence at Luxemburg, for there was something chill and foreboding about Schönbrunn. A splendid palace, built in the previous century by her illustrious great-aunt Marie Antoinette and boasting over twelve hundred rooms of gilded, ornate magnificence, it nevertheless held an air of menace for the child and she had never been able to sleep there without the comfort of a light. Sometimes in the night she had sensed a strange, chill presence hovering close, but she had never had the courage to peep out from under the blankets to discover what it was.

But tonight she had no warning of its coming. In the small hours of the night she awoke suddenly, feeling clammy sweat standing on her cold skin, and there in the sombre light of the candle stood the figure of a woman, close to the foot of the bed.

She was ethereally pale and expressionless, and in horror Marie Louise realized she could see through her to the great clothes press beyond. Slowly, deliberately, the white lady turned and walked towards the wall, disappearing like a breath of steam as she reached it.

Marie Louise lay sick with terror, then flung herself from the bed and rushed for the door, screaming for Aja.

'What is it, child?' Madame Colloredo sat upright in bed, her hair in curl-papers. Marie Louise barely noticed Aja's husband the Count, still fully-dressed in his uniform as the Emperor's *aide de camp* who sat on the edge of the bed. She hurled herself, weeping, upon Madame and babbled out an incoherent tale of the White Lady. Aja listened, and Marie Louise saw the interchange of looks between her and her husband. Aja's arms were warmly reassuring.

'Come now, sweetheart, let me tuck you into bed again, and I shall leave the door open between us,' she said after Marie Louise's sobs had abated. 'It was but a nightmare and all is well now.'

Comforted, Marie Louise followed her obediently back to her own chamber. But sleep did not return, and after a time she could hear Aja's voice murmuring low, and the Count's mumbled replies.

'It is an evil omen, husband.'

'Nonsense. Mere superstition, my dear.'

'That may be so, but the White Lady has been seen in Schönbrunn before, and each time her appearance has presaged tragedy. The Emperor himself saw it when he was still Crown Prince—no less than twice, if the servants are to be believed.'

'That proves nothing.'

'I wonder. The first time he saw it his first wife the Archduchess Elizabeth sickened and died, and the second time his uncle the Emperor Joseph died.'

Marie Louise heard Count Colloredo's sardonic laugh. 'That was no tragedy for Emperor Francis, my dear, for did he not then inherit the Holy Roman Crown? And as to his wife Elizabeth's death, why. . . . You did not know him then, but I was his governor in his youth and have watched him develop. A woman to him is a creature to enjoy, to use to the full, as Elizabeth soon discovered. She died bearing his child, and the Empress Maria Theresa, too, is rapidly being worn away from his insatiable lust.'

Marie Louise lay awake in the darkness, unable to grasp the meaning of his words, save that he did not approve and love her father as unreservedly as she did, for there was criticism of the Emperor implicit in his tone. He spoke again, and this time there was affectionate teasing in his voice.

'You are a gullible soul, are you not? A child's nightmare has you believing evil is to come just when I believe I have the Emperor on the right path at last. No doubt you will tell me you also believe the servants' tale about the Empress and the fortune-teller who foresaw it in the cards many years ago in Naples that she would marry a widower and die at thirty-four?'

Aja's voice was low, but Marie Louise could just discern her words.

'Well, it has partially come true, has it not?'

'She married a widower, yes, but die at thirty-four? You know her age now? She is thirty-three, and despite constant pregnancies she is fit and well. Do you truly give credence to such a superstition, wife?'

There was silence for a moment, and then Aja's voice murmured, 'I do not know, my dear. I only know I feel this strange sense of unease.'

Count Colloredo's gentle laughter echoed into Marie Louise's room, and then the door between closed softly.

So anxious was the Emperor Francis, once aroused, to overcome the French tyrant that he acted with characteristic impulsiveness, hurling his army into Bavaria without waiting for his Russian allies to come to his aid. Bonaparte responded equally swiftly, crossing the Rhine to force back the Austrian General Mack and obliging him to surrender at Ulm. The chill of approaching winter in Vienna grew yet more chill when news came that the Monster, wrathful and resolved, was marching on towards the capital.

Aja's face was sickly green with fear as she hurried to Marie Louise. 'Come, let us hasten to pack, Louise, for the French army is as near as Dirnstein. The family is to flee Vienna at once.'

Marie Louise stared blankly. 'But whither, Aja?'

'Your Mama the Empress is to take little Leopoldine to Bohemia, and you and Ferdi and Caroline and the others are to travel to Hungary, to the safety of Count Esterhazy's château in Kittsee. Come, there is no time to lose.'

The palace was in confusion, servants scurrying hither and thither, creaking coaches at the doors hastily loaded with trunks and boxes and bags, and the family tearfully making their farewells of each other. Ferdi whined in fright, Marie Louise saw to her disgust. At twelve he was too big to cry, even if the awful bogeyman who had plagued his whole childhood was at last on the verge of appearing in person.

But Marie Louise too wept, to be separated from her numerous brothers and sisters. A final glimpse into her pet-house, to blow a kiss to her adored collection of rabbits and doves and pigeons.

'I shall return, my beauties, just so soon as the Monster is gone,' she promised them, before hastening back to where Aja paced, impatiently waiting by the coach.

'Where is Victoire, Aja?' Marie Louise's voice was shrill and anxious.

'She is to be taken to safety, have no fear. Now hurry.'

'But I must write her a note!' And refusing to mount before it was done, Marie Louise ran back into the palace.

'I am in despair to leave without saying goodbye to my dear, sweet Victoire. Pray hard that the good God may reunite us. I kiss you over and over again, and in spite of all the sorrows in this world, I shall always remain your attached friend.

Louise.'

That done, she climbed aboard the carriage content. The journey was a long and hazardous one. For weeks they travelled, becoming more and more weary and dishevelled, staying in lodgings which varied from fine houses to shoddy, lice-ridden inns, but to pause was more than they dared. Napoleon Bonaparte's troops marched relentlessly on, always victorious.

'The Ogre dwells now in Schönbrunn,' Aja told the young Archduchess sorrowfully as the coach bumped onwards into Hungary. Marie Louise shivered. It seemed sacrilegious to think of that foul Corsican creature defiling the royal sanctity of the home of Hapsburg Kings.

'It is reported to me that he even sleeps in your chamber, Your Highness. It seems now that the warning of the White Lady was for a very good reason, Louise.'

Marie Louise was shocked. To think of that Beast lying in her bed! From infancy she had been protected from male company, none being allowed near her save her tutor, Herr Kotzeluch, and her bodyservants. Even her pets were all carefully selected, the female of the species only being allowed to inhabit her pet-house. A man, and a filthy Corsican peasant at that, in the intimacy of her bed! It was unthinkable!

'You believe the White Lady was forewarning us of the Beast's coming, Aja?' Marie Louise ventured timidly.

Aja nodded. 'And more trouble beside. Do you know that the Emperor blames my husband the Count for the army's bad fortunes of late?"

'Oh, surely not, Aja!'

'As Minister of State the Count is held responsible. I fear your Papa may punish him, dismiss him even.'

'Oh, no, Aja! We all love you and the Count! Papa would not do that!'

Madame Colloredo leaned across, taking Marie Louise's hands in her own. 'Perhaps your word would persuade your Papa we serve him well, Louise. Your father loves you dearly.'

'I know it, Aja, and I him.'

'As do the Count and myself. Perhaps you would write to him? And a commending word to Mama the Empress would not come amiss either?'

'To be sure, Mama Colloredo! I shall write just as soon as we arrive at Count Esterhazy's.'

But Louise's entreaties and the Countess's subtlety were of no avail. Anxious to find a scapegoat for his failure, the Emperor dismissed Count Colloredo. Marie Louise, in her guileless simplicity, could have swallowed her disappointment, but not the terrible blow which ensued. At the Esterhazy château she waited for news from home, yearning to hear that the Beast had been ousted from Vienna.

Aja burst into the chamber, frenzied and uncontrolled. Marie Louise stared. The Countess, usually so composed and dignified, was sobbing noisily, tearing to shreds the handkerchief in her hands.

'Louise, my love! All is undone!'

Fear clutched Marie Louise's heart. 'What is it, Aja?'

'Your father—not content with spurning the Count who loved him well—now plans to remove me from you! I cannot bear it, Louise, I who have loved and cared for you so long!' Sobs again wracked the heartbroken woman, rage and grief vying with each other in her tumultuous passion.

The Archduchess shrieked. 'Remove you? Oh no, Aja! That cannot be! My father would not be so cruel to me!'

'It is your mother who persuades him, beloved. She is convinced I am an evil influence on you. She thinks I use you to further my own ends. Oh Louise! How could she!'

The older woman wept bitterly, while Marie Louise stood aghast, barely able to comprehend. She could not visualise life without this woman who had been mother, friend and supporter to her all these years. It was cruel, unbelievable!

'I will write to Papa . . .' she mumbled at last.

'To no avail, my sweet. The Count is disgraced and I must share his dishonour. They have appointed another aja, a Frau von Faber, to care for you.'

Marie Louise flung herself into Mama Colloredo's arms, weeping hysterically. 'But I want you, Aja, I need you! You cannot leave me.'

Aja held her at arm's length and looked down into the tear-fringed blue eyes. She smiled warmly. 'She cannot love you as I do, sweetheart. Remember that—wherever I am, we are never separated because there is no distance between where love and prayers unite.'

And though both the young girl and the woman wailed and wept, heartbrokenly they parted. The Empress Maria Theresa's new choice of governess arrived, the Frau von Faber, and Marie Louise tried to compose herself into a state of acceptance. Sorrowfully she wrote to her mother.

'I hope and I adjure you, dearest mother, that you will forget the thoughtless Louise and see only the submissive one who is devoted to her parents.'

There, now she felt better. Though separation from Aja and dear Victoire was heartrending, there was comfort to be gained from endeavouring to please her parents. And perhaps now Mama would soften towards her and show her a little love?

Word came that Mama was sick, abed in Olmütz, but at the enemy's approach she was forced to rise in order to flee, over icy, rutted roads, to the border. Marie Louise prayed earnestly for her safety, and it seemed God listened, for the Empress recovered.

But another blow was in store. Beloved Papa's army, meeting the French in a dense mist near Austerlitz, was miserably defeated and Papa, to save his Empire from utter ruin, was obliged to bend his pride and sue the Corsican for peace. Near the Mill of Poleny he met the upstart, and the Treaty of Pressburg was agreed. It was Christmas, 1805. Papa, she was told, was no longer Emperor of the Holy Roman Empire, but only of a vastly-diminished Austria. Marie Louise wept tears of shame and misery for him.

The only consolation was that, now that the fighting was over, she could return to Vienna and be reunited with her family. Marie Louise felt her normally sunny optimism returning. Life would be empty and very different without Aja and Victoire, but it would be wonderful to have the little ones running about again, and her pets, and of course, Papa. . . .

Of the Monster there was no sign. He had departed from Schönbrunn as if he had never been. In her chamber Marie Louise found her clothes-presses and cupboards undisturbed; he had not been so disgusting as to rifle among her precious, personal possessions. The only evidence of any intrusion was a scarcely-detectable scent of eau-de-cologne mingled with jasmine.

One heard from time to time that he was doling out European kingdoms to his family. Not content with usurping the Bourbon throne for himself, he made his brother Louis, King of Holland and his brother Joseph, King of Naples—grandmother's kingdoms. Brother Jerome he planned to marry into royal blood, creating him King of Westphalia. There was no end to the upstart's ambition.

With the coming of spring Vienna's natural air of *joie de vivre* seemed to be returning at last. Marie Louise began to feel contented once more, life, with the new Aja Faber and the new Comptroller Esterhazy, having an air of stability and peace.

On Mama's birthday in June, Marie Louise involuntarily

recalled the murmured conversation overheard in the night so long ago, of the gipsy's prediction that the Empress would die at thirty-four. Nonsense, thought the young Archduchess contentedly. Mama is thirty-four now and looks as fit and well as ever she did. The White Lady brought enough trouble, what with flight and defeat and the loss of Aja and Victoire. . . . Now all was going to be well, she was sure of it.

But once again Marie Louise's trusting faith in Providence was to be swiftly shattered.

CHAPTER 3

VIENNA, 1807–1809

NOT long after the Empress's birthday it was announced that she was again *enceinte*. In the spring she was to expect her thirteenth child. For the fifteen-year-old Archduchess Marie Louise a new arrival was by now a regular occurrence, but how and why these little brothers and sisters came to be, was of no import. She neither knew nor questioned her own ignorance, for it was sufficient that these delightful creatures appeared.

Marie Louise dined often in her parents' State apartments now, accompanied by Ferdinand, now thirteen and treated with deference as the Crown Prince and heir-apparent to the Austrian throne. Papa seemed edgy and often irritable at dinner, annoyed by Mama's constant weariness and disinclination to chat.

'I am to go on progress through Hungary shortly, Maria, and would welcome your company. You have not been anywhere with me of late,' he commented one evening.

Maria Theresa passed a languid hand across her forehead. 'If you will permit, I would prefer to remain at home, my dear,' she answered weakly. 'I feel no energy, and my time is not far distant.'

Papa clicked his tongue in exasperation. 'You never go anywhere with me now. I should not be surprised if the rumour grew that we were estranged.'

'Nonsense, my dear.' Maria's smile was feeble. 'With the advent of our thirteenth child, who could be so foolish as to believe that?'

Marie Louise surveyed her mother critically. How could she refuse Papa his request? True, she did look somewhat pale and drawn—but then, she always did.

Papa rode away, the Archduchess waving goodbye sadly from an upper window. Beloved Papa, she thought, time will drag slowly until you are back home again. . . .

One night Marie Louise awoke suddenly and knew by the cold sweat on her skin that the presence was here again. Turning fearful eyes towards the bed-end, she gasped. The woman in white, veil flowing from her head, stood looking at her sorrowfully, and then suddenly vanished. Terrified, Marie Louise leapt and ran screaming to her mother's room. Maria Theresa lay still and pallid in her vast empty bed.

'You saw her too?' her thin voice questioned.

'The White Lady, Mama! I saw her again!' Marie Louise crawled into the bed and lay shivering next to her mother, but there was no warmth to be gleaned from her, for she was ice-cold.

'She came to me also.' The Empress's voice was flat and emotionless.

'Are you not afraid, Mama?'

'What will be, will be. There is nothing you or I can do to change it,' the stark voice answered. Marie Louise lay, disbelieving and terrified. What was this terrible thing, this spectre which could render her mother so lifeless and drained of emotion? Oh, if only Papa were here, with his great strength and comfort to drive away the apparition and the terror it engendered!

Mama was pale but composed next morning, but in the evening there was a great flurry about her apartments, servants and doctors bursting past Marie Louise, but not one pausing to explain to her what was occurring.

'Let me go to Mama," she begged Aja Faber.

'Not now, child. She has pain and it is believed the child is coming.'

'But she needs me, Aja!'

'You will be in the way, Your Highness. The physicians are bleeding her, and your Papa has been sent for, so have no fear. Soon all will be well.'

But before the Emperor pounded into the Palace the Empress was delivered of a fragile tiny girl. Papa brushed Marie Louise aside in his haste to go to his wife, and again the young Archduchess found herself excluded from the bed-chamber.

Three days passed, At length Aja announced solemnly that Marie Louise and Ferdinand could go in to the Empress. Marie Louise approached the bed timidly. Mama lay motion-less and pallid, only her eyes searching brightly about her. Papa sat nearby, his head bent and clutching the Empress's pale limp hand in his own. Marie Louise felt tears pricking her eyes. Ferdinand hung back, gauche and nervous.

Great lustrous eyes turned upon them. 'Come closer, my children,' Mama's frail voice said. 'Ferdinand, my son, let me warn you, when you come to rule in your father's place, choose to have about you men of brains and piety, but never those who have one without the other.'

Her words hung on the darkening air like mist, tenuous and fleeting. With sudden certainty Marie Louise knew she was dying.

'And you, Louise,' the faint voice added, 'remember your duty and obedience always. It is woman's crowning virtue, and especially a royal woman's.'

'I will, Mama.' Marie Louise knelt by the bed and took

the cold, white fingers in hers, feeling the chill of death in them. Mama smiled weakly. Somehow, in death, Marie Louise felt that her mother, ever undemonstrative and aloof, was closer to her and more loving than ever before. Tears fell from the girl's eyes. 'Bless me, Mama,' she whispered hoarsely.

The pale fingers lifted slowly, traced the sign of the cross on Marie Louise's bowed forehead, and fell limply. Papa nodded to Marie Louise and Ferdinand to leave.

The Archduchess did not see her mother again. One final glimpse as she lay, white-shrouded, in her coffin, and then she was borne away to the gloomy Hapsburg vault in the crypt of the Capucin chapel. Marie Louise found no time for despair and self-pity, for her father was near-hysterical with shock at his sudden loss. Crazed with grief he shambled about the Palace aimlessly, oblivious both of his duties and of his eight surviving motherless children.

His physicians ordered a change of air and of scene. 'A progress through your states, Your Imperial Highness,' they advised.

'I cannot travel alone,' he moaned forlornly.

And so it was he turned to his eldest child, his sixteen-year-old daughter Marie Louise for comfort and support.

'Come with me, Luischen, I need you,' he pleaded.

'To be sure, Papa. I will do anything I can to please and console you,' she replied willingly.

And indeed she was glad to be of help to him in his need, her adored Father. It was wonderful to have him to herself, and the journey was sheer joy to her. She wrote often to Victoire of her contentment.

'These journeys interest me greatly, because my dear Papa is so kind as to instruct me in a multitude of things; but each place we go everything reminds us of our terrible loss.'

For several months, however, Papa seemed content with her company even after their return to Vienna, and then suddenly he seemed to tire of it. It is because I am immature and unsophisticated, Marie Louise fretted, a far from adequate substitute for Maria with her wit and wisdom. The atmosphere was funereal still, with black crepe gowns and weary ceremonial. He needs a brighter, more refreshing atmosphere and more congenial, sparkling company.

But it came as a shock, nevertheless, to find Papa was evidently thinking likewise, for he began searching around among royal princesses to select a new wife for himself. Marie Louise felt saddened. What was there a wife could offer Papa that she could not?

One of the many visitors to Schönbrunn Palace at the time was the Dowager Archduchess Beatrix of Este-Modena who, with her husband and children, had been driven from her Italian estates a few years previously by Napoleon. Her husband Duke Ferdinand was Emperor Francis' uncle, but soon after their arrival in Vienna, the Duke died. The Archduchess lived now in Vienna with her as-yet unmarried daughter, the lively twenty-year-old Maria Ludovica. At Schönbrunn Marie Louise watched the pretty, piquant face of Maria Ludovica as she talked animatedly, and heard others speak of her quick, clever brain. She was a delightful girl, Marie Louise thought, only four years older than herself. What a charming companion she would make!

Papa was in one of his morose moods again. He was not sleeping well, he said, and no doubt that accounted for his abrupt manner and sometimes muddled behaviour. At dinner tonight he was unusually taciturn and everyone, sensing the atmosphere, ate in silence with occasional nervous glances in his direction. Ferdinand looked meaningfully across the table at Marie Louise, and none dared break the silence.

The silence became strained, fraught with tension. Now and again Papa sighed deeply. It was young brother Karl who at last dared to break the ominous silence.

'Are you ill, Papa?'

Marie Louise watched. Every eye in the room was focused on the Emperor. Growing redder and redder, he at length flung down his napkin on the table.

'Ill, fool? Of course I am ill!' he roared. 'How can I be well without a wife?'

No one spoke. No one dared. It was not a question but a statement of an overwhelmingly obvious fact in the Emperor's eyes. Timidly Marie Louise picked up her fork and continued eating.

And then he announced his choice. 'I have chosen to marry Maria Ludovica,' he announced firmly, and with that he swept from the dining room. Marie Louise sat, numb, the fork motionless in her hand. Marie Ludovica, twenty years his junior and again his first cousin, just as Maria Theresa had been, was to become his third bride.

'Perhaps it is as well,' Ferdinand commented. 'He is unbearably moody without a woman.'

'I believed he found his love for us was sufficient,' Marie Louise murmured miserably. Ferdinand laughed.

'Enough for Papa? You do not know him, Louise. He needs a bed-mate as well as a soulmate. Perhaps now he will revert to normal once he is wed. Besides, she's not a bad choice, clever and capable, and her hatred of Napoleon Bonaparte is renowned.'

'Is that good, Ferdi?'

'Yes. Papa needs a strong mind to guide him.'

'But it is so sudden. Maria has not been dead for many months. It is not—fitting.'

'Papa will tell you the smaller children need a mother, Louise.'

'Yes, I suppose so. But I am not happy about this marriage.'

'You cannot dissuade him.'

'But I can try! Yes, I *will* try! I'll go to him and plead with him!' Marie Louise was near to tears.

Ferdi smiled. 'Jealous, Luischen? No, I am sorry. Go by all means, but he will not listen. He needs a woman desperately, and I fear it is a role you cannot fulfil.'

Nevertheless Marie Louise was determined. She walked with resolution towards Papa's study, but at the door she faltered. It was so uncharacteristic of her to argue, to refute. All her life she had been a model of submission and compliance, and it tried her conscience to enter a debate with her father now. But she was a woman now, sixteen and fully-grown, and so much was at stake. Suppose this Maria Ludovica had deliberately set out to snare Papa, to advance herself for her own ends? They said she hated Bonaparte—suppose she hoped now to induce Papa to provoke the Monster again, as they once said Count Colloredo had done?

And so much more was at stake. Marie Louise needed Papa's love; all his children did. A strange woman might alienate him from them. Marie Louise knocked at the study door.

'Enter.'

Papa was sitting at his desk. As etiquette demanded, Marie Louise advanced, curtseyed and kissed his hand. Papa eyed her curiously.

'What is it, Luischen? Do you come to congratulate me on my coming nuptials?'

Marie Louise hung her head. 'No, Papa.'

'No? Then what is it brings you here?'

The fair young head tilted high again. 'I come to plead with you not to marry Maria Ludovica, Papa.'

His face darkened. 'Go on,' he commanded.

'I do not think it is proper, when it is not yet six months since Mama died. Moreover I believe it is your duty to us, to all of us children, to grant your love and comfort to us. You cannot forget your children by allowing this woman to come between us.'

'Can I not?' The voice was low and menacing. 'Have you anything more to say, Louise?'

'Only that I will not accept her as my stepmother.' Marie Louise's voice faltered. She had not meant to sound so insolently dictatorial. Papa rose slowly from his chair, and Marie Louise's heart leapt with hope. He was coming round to embrace her and reassure her!

But instead he crossed to the door in silence, opening it and standing back to glare at her. Without a word he pointed firmly out into the corridor, and submissively Marie Louise went out, hurt and defeat and bitter disappointment filling her eyes with scalding tears. In the doorway his ice-cold voice halted her.

'Let me say just this, daughter. The first time I was married it was to please my uncle the Emperor; the second time was to please my father; *this* time I plan to please myself. Goodnight.'

So it was that, eight months after Maria Theresa's death, Emperor Francis took Maria Ludovica to wife. Marie Louise regarded her new stepmother with suspicion mingled with jealousy, but the older girl sensed the family's antipathy and went out of her way to woo their affection. Marie Louise could not hold out against her; the young stepmother was so laughing and lovely, so frail in appearance and so appealing that gradually she found her animosity melting. In time she grew to like Maria Ludovica well, especially as the charm of the girl seemed to be having the desired effect of mellowing Papa and restoring him to his erstwhile equanimity.

'She is not unpleasant after all,' Marie Louise admitted to Ferdinand reluctantly. 'I grow to like her well.'

Ferdi grunted. 'She is clever. She has Papa in the palm of her hand and, if she has her way, we shall be at war with France again before long.'

'Oh no! Surely not!' Marie Louise gasped

Ferdi's blue eyes probed hers questioningly. 'Do you not see how she fills our court with dispossessed French émigrés? Was not her own mother usurped by the tyrant? She will not hesitate to persuade Papa to take arms against a man she loathes as much as she does Napoleon Bonaparte.'

'No, no, Ferdi. I think you mistake her,' Marie Louise remonstrated. 'See how much life and gaiety she has brought to our Court. Much of the stuffy old etiquette has vanished since she came, so much it is enlivened by the Court balls and entertainments she has arranged. So many young people she has invited here, for our benefit, I am sure.'

'To cast around for a likely husband for you, no doubt,' Ferdi answered gruffly. Marie Louise stared.

'What is that you say?'

'You are sixteen and highly marriageable. Do you think she wants a pretty girl to remain in her Court to rival her? No, mark my words, my dear sister, it is a husband for you and a war against France she seeks, or I am much mistaken.'

His sister stared aghast. Either Ferdi was an incredibly astute young man and she a gullible fool, or he spoke with malice. But when rumours began to fly that Maria Ludovica was advocating her unpleasant young brother Francesco to the Emperor as a suitable match for Marie Louise, the young Archduchess held her breath in fear.

Relief came only when she heard Papa would have none of it. Marie Louise could breathe again, for the thought of being united with that ghastly Francesco had been anathema to her.

Bonaparte was having trouble in Spain. The new Empress, thwarted of one ambition, implored her husband to attack the now vulnerable Corsican, and foolishly he agreed. In front of the great Hofburg Palace Marie Louise watched the ceremony of the Blessing of the Standards and then stared sadly as Papa rode away, resplendent in his magnificent military uniform. But very soon came the news that the French army was beating him back. While Marie Louise felt fear for his safety, his young wife's eyes simply gleamed the more brightly with hatred of the Monster.

Papa's army retreated towards Vienna, the French army in close pursuit. Anxiously the Empress gave orders for the Imperial Family, now residing in the great Hofburg Palace, to pack and flee instantly to the safety of Hungary.

Marie Louise felt sick at heart. Now, in 1809, it seemed it was to be 1805 and ignominious flight all over again. Wearily she watched the lumbering coaches being hastily filled with trunks again. Once more the Ogre of France was putting to flight her beloved family. It was so unfair. Would virtue and piety never succeed in triumphing over evil? With the prospect of furtive flight from inn to flea-ridden inn for maybe weeks stretching miserably before her, Marie Louise felt her head begin to spin and her knees to weaken under her. . . .

When she opened her eyes again she could see the burgeoning spring buds on the trees outside the Palace windows. She was lying in bed, Maria Ludovica and the physicians murmuring at the foot of the bed.

'I would advise that the Archduchess is not moved at this moment,' the doctor was saying. 'She has a fever and movement could be critical.'

'But we must go!' the Empress's voice urged. 'When will she be fit to travel?'

'Not for three or four days at least. I would advise, Your Highness that you and your family leave at once, and my colleagues and I will tend the Archduchess.'

'Delay would be dangerous,' Maria Ludovica agreed. 'If you are certain the enemy will not harm her if they come. . . .'

'They will not, madame. And we shall arrange for her to follow you to Buda when she is sufficiently recovered.'

The voices faded into a haze and Marie Louise remembered no more. When she recovered consciousness again it was to the dull sound of gunfire and the crack of exploding shells. She struggled to sit upright. A pale, tense doctor hurried into the room.

'Lie still, Your Highness. You have been very ill,' he urged.

'But that noise—my family—where is Papa?'

'The Emperor is still away on the battlefield. Your family have fled to safety some days ago.'

Rumbles and hoarse cries could be heard outside. Marie Louise gazed blankly at the doctor. 'And is that sound—is it the French who bombard Vienna?'

The doctor nodded solemnly. 'I fear so, Your Highness. It cannot be long before Vienna falls, and then Bonaparte will march in.'

The spectre of the Ogre, the Monster she and Ferdi had tried so hard to annihilate all those years ago in Schönbrunn nursery, rose grey and threatening before Marie Louise's fevered eyes. With a cry of utter fear and helplessness she once more lost consciousness. . . .

CHAPTER 4

VIENNA, 1809

MARIE LOUISE was unaware of the thudding hoofbeats of the French soldiers as they rode into Vienna, for she lay still sick and delirious in her bed in the Hofburg Palace. Nor did she learn until much later that Bonaparte, on hearing that the Archduchess lay ill within the city, had ordered the roar of bombardment to cease and had taken up residence in Schönbrunn Palace instead of in the Hofburg. All this she learned only when she had recovered and was travelling towards Hungary and her family.

'That was indeed kindly of Bonaparte,' she mused aloud.

'Kindly indeed!' snorted the Empress. 'I hear he brought his Polish doxy to share his pleasure in Schönbrunn. He would not wish to affront true royal blood by disporting before you, he a Corsican peasant and she a Countess no better than she ought to be! She left her husband, that fickle Marie Walewska, to be with her lover in our beautiful Schönbrunn! How disgusting!'

It took the whole summer before an armistice was signed between defeated Austria and France. Napoleon Bonaparte stayed in Schönbrunn, demanding oppressive and humiliating terms which the Emperor Francis was not prepared to concede and Marie Louise wept to hear of his misery and disgrace.

Marie Louise wrote to Madame Colloredo:

'I assure you I am turned to stone, so much have I already suffered by the war. It seems to me our family is not made for happy days, and all the same Papa does so deserve them.'

It was even rumoured the Monster intended to depose Papa and put Marie Louise's uncle, the Grand Duke of Würzburg, in his place. Marie Louise, like all the royal family, awaited the outcome nervously.

'I hear that Bonaparte intends to make a tour of the States,' Victoire wrote to her one day.

'I only pray that he may keep far away,' Marie Louise wrote back. 'I assure you that to see that person would be a torment worse than all the martyrdoms.'

At length in the autumn Francis, now weary of all the strife and delay, yielded to the conquering tyrant's harsh terms. His ministers advised it : 'The existence of the Austrian monarchy is at stake, but the dissolution of the French Empire is not far off.'

So with the Peace of Vienna enriching France by some fifty thousand miles of Austrian territory, the victorious Napoleon Bonaparte returned to Paris. Marie Louise and her family were free to return to Vienna. All about them they heard their Austrian subjects muttering imprecations against the hated, predatory French. In December Marie Louise celebrated her eighteenth birthday. Slowly life in the capital seemed to be picking up its former routine once more. Fine carriages reappeared to rumble leisurely along the Prater and people strolled in the winter sunshine to offer their thanksgiving for peace in the churches.

It was the new year, 1810. Marie Louise found the Empress reclining on a sofa reading the 'Moniteur.'

'Have you read of Bonaparte's latest action?' she enquired of her stepdaughter lazily. Marie Louise's heart lurched.

'Not another campaign, surely?'

Maria Ludovica laughed shortly. 'Not a military one this time, my dear. No. He plans to divorce the Empress Josephine.'

'Divorce her? But why?'

Stepmother eyed her curiously. 'Because she has given him no son, and it is essential for Bonaparte's ambition that he has a son to succeed him.'

Marie Louise reflected. 'It seems strange, when they have been wed so many years. Everyone believed he loved her. Why divorce her now, I wonder?'

'Because his lover Marie Walewska has borne him a son, proving beyond doubt he is not sterile. Although Josephine had two children by her earlier marriage, she has conceived none during her fourteen years of marriage to Bonaparte, so she must go.'

'How cruel!' Marie Louise exclaimed.

'There is more to it than that, Maria Ludovica explained. 'Josephine is of base origin like himself, a Creole. It would be far better for Bonaparte's plans to take himself a wife of royal blood who is fertile into the bargain. Before long he will be searching Europe for a royal bride.'

Clammy fingers seemed to grip Marie Louise's heart. She had a hazy feeling that she began to understand the drift of her stepmother's careful explanations. Normally Maria Ludovica did not spend so much time in political conversation with Marie Louise. However, the Empress swiftly turned the conversation into another, lighter channel.

Ferdi was laconic on the subject. 'It seems likely the Ogre will indeed seek a royal bride,' he agreed.

'But who, Ferdi? Not an Archduchess surely? Would he

dare seek the Grand Duchess Anne of Russia, do you think?'
Marie Louise could not bring herself to voice the terrible fear
that lurked in her heart.

Ferdi shrugged. 'He is brazen enough. And his chosen bride
will have little choice. Catherine of Württemberg was obliged
to marry his brother Jerome when he willed it, whether she
liked it or not.'

Speculation buzzed, both in Vienna and every other
court in Europe. Daily, Marie Louise opened the newspaper
in trepidation, hopeful and yet fearful of reading the
announcement as to the Monster's choice.

He would not ask for her hand, surely. He might seek Tsar
Alexander's young sister Anne, but never Marie Louise of
Austria—would he? It was true she and Anne were the only
two Imperial princesses in Europe, but surely he could not
dare? Throughout her life Marie Louise had known her husband would not be of her choosing, for princesses were not
free to choose—but Papa would never permit such a terrible
thing to happen to his favoured child. Desperately she took
refuge from her unspoken fear in this consoling thought. Only
to Madame Colloredo and Victoire did she hint of the fear
that possessed her.

'Since Napoleon's divorce,' she wrote, 'I open every
Frankfurt newspaper in the hope of learning whether the
new wife has yet been named. The delay makes me uneasy.'

Speculation and gossip gave rise to rumours, that Napoleon
had sought Anne of Russia only to be refused. It was further
reported that Anne's mother, the Empress Catherine, had
declared she would sooner see her daughter drowned in the
River Neva than handed over to the Ogre. Marie Louise
shivered in dread. No, her fears must be unfounded! No one,
especially Papa, had yet suggested she could be the victim!

She was mad to believe Papa would permit his hated rival to claim a Hapsburg bride, and she his adored daughter!

The terrified Archduchess considered pleading with Maria Ludovica, failing a mother to protect her, but the Empress suddenly fell ill. It would be useless anyway, Marie Louise reflected, for though Maria Ludovica hated Napoleon Bonaparte with a fierce bitterness, she would undoubtedly agree to an alliance which would give Austria his protection. Austria desperately needed a few years of peace after so many spent in warring, depriving her of all her strength. Marie Louise wept alone and waited.

Her name began to be spoken audibly in connection with Bonaparte. It was her tutor, Kotzeluch, who was the one who finally said it in her presence, as she sat one evening at her desk, writing to Victoire. Marie Louise closed her ears, willing the horrifying idea to take flight, but could not resist observing to Victoire: 'I hear Kotzeluch talking about Napoleon's divorce. I heard him say that I have been picked as the successor, but he is mistaken there. Papa is far too kind to constrain me in so important a matter.'

Within days more voices were mentioning her name. Marie Louise wrote stubbornly:

'I let people talk, and do not concern myself with what they say. I only pity the princess whom he will choose, for I shall certainly not be made a victim of politics.'

The whispering grew, and Papa remained pale and silent. The Empress, now recovering from her sickness, spent much time closeted in conversation with him. Marie Louise's determination to hold out against fate began to waver, and she picked up her pen to write plaintively to Madame Colloredo.

'If misfortune demands it, I am ready to sacrifice my personal happiness for the good of the State. I do not want to think any more about it. But my mind is made up, although it will be a double and very painful sacrifice. Pray that it may not be!'

The reflection in the mirror stared back at her, pale and drawn. No longer could she eat as heartily as she always had; nightly sleep eluded her. Dark apparitions milled in her over-wrought brain, and Marie Louise sobbed for want of a friend in whom to confide. If only Grandmother were still here, but she had returned to her own kingdom of Sicily. Would there be no end to these endless weeks of anguished uncertainty?

It was the Empress who brought hope to Marie Louise. 'Why do you not tell your Papa that you would like to marry my brother Francesco after all?' she suggested. 'Tell him you have fallen in love, then perhaps he will not force you to wed where you do not wish it.'

The Emperor Francis' reply was emphatic. To his wife he said tersely, 'Francesco has nothing, you have nothing, I have nothing and the girl has nothing. Pray what kind of a marriage will that make?'

Marie Louise's heart sank. That avenue of escape was blocked. Unpleasant as marriage with Francesco would have been, it was as nothing compared to the threat of being wedded to the Ogre. Marie Louise remembered with horror the fate of the last bride who had travelled forth from Vienna to marry and rule over the French. Great-aunt Marie Antoinette forty years before had left Vienna joyously, only to lose her lovely head under the guillotine in Paris. Oddly enough, there was no mention of ill-fated Marie Antoinette in the Hofburg now that another Austrian princess was apparently about to follow in her footsteps.

It was curious that there happened to be staying in Vienna at this moment two eminent Frenchmen, the Comte de Narbonne, who was on his way to Munich to take up his post as French Minister Plenipotentiary, and the Prince de Ligne. Both, moreover, were being handsomely entertained by Count Metternich, the wily Austrian Foreign Minister. But these events held no meaning at all for the simple Archduchess. It was only when her father summoned her to his study one morning that she realized the significance of the foreign guests' presence in Vienna.

'Pray be seated, Louise,' Papa said gently, then turned away to gaze out of the window. Marie Louise sat, waiting in silence as protocol demanded, until the Emperor spoke. He seemed to be in no hurry to begin, his hands thrust deep in his pockets as he stared at the bleak winter sky outside. Marie Louise was still thinking of her young sister Leopoldine's curious stare when someone mentioned yet again Napoleon's possible choice of a bride, and of her own retort.

'If the Monster had intended to ask for my hand,' she had burst out, 'he would surely have done so by now. Thank God, I feel the danger has passed.'

That had been just a few moments ago, just before the summons to Papa's study came. Marie Louise looked across at his averted back and wondered why he had sent for her, an unusual occurrence. He turned and stared at her listlessly, bleakness staring out of his eyes.

'You know, my daughter, that as members of an ancient royal line, it is often our duty to do that which, while unpleasant, is yet our duty and therefore must be our satisfaction.' It was a statement, boldly and tonelessly made. Marie Louise inclined her head in agreement, wondering what was to come.

The Emperor came a step closer, raised a hand as though to caress her shoulder, then dropped it and looked at the tapestried wall beyond her as he continued to speak.

'Count Metternich has just left me. He tells me he spoke long and earnestly last night with the Comte de Narbonne and the Prince de Ligne. The Comte was of the opinion there soon would be but two Empires in Europe, the one French and the other either Austria or Russia.'

He paused, turning away again to stare at the mantelshelf. Marie Louise, deeming it appropriate to speak now since he remained silent, looked up meekly.

'I am happy you see fit to instruct me in international affairs, Papa, for I confess I am ignorant on many matters. But to what end do you consult me? Would not the Empress be better able to converse with you on these matters? I fear I can be of little help.'

The Emperor rounded quickly, his eyes afire now. 'But that is where you are mistaken, Luischen. You can be of inestimable value to me—to Austria—if you will.'

'I? But how?'

'Austria is in danger. With no army we are defenceless. The Treaty of Vienna is in jeopardy unless it is strengthened by another bond, a more intimate alliance. The Comte has made it clear that Austria has it in her power to become the other Empire alongside France to rule Europe if we will but take the step.'

'What step, Papa?' Despite the innocence of the words Marie Louise's heart froze. She had a blinding, terrifying premonition of what he was about to say. Oh no, Papa, you could not ask it of me!

'Bonaparte seeks an Imperial bride. To accept his hand would render Austria safe.' His voice was faint and far-away. His eyes gazed at her blankly. Marie Louise's senses swam, and she caught at the arm of her chair to steady herself.

'You—wish me to marry Napoleon Bonaparte?' Her voice

croaked as she spoke the words, reluctant to hear it confirmed that her beloved Papa wished this dreadful thing of her.

'Do not give me your answer now, child. Go and think on it. But remember, it is you who must decide. I shall never force you. Go now and leave me to think.'

He kept his face averted as Marie Louise made her obeisance and left the room. Waves of dizziness still engulfed her as she stumbled back to the sanctuary of her own room. Sweeping up her beloved dog Bijou into her arms, she sobbed unrestrainedly into his shaggy fur. Oh Papa! How could you wish such misery and degradation upon your beloved child, she wept. It was the greatest disillusionment of all.

Sleep came belatedly that night to the wretched Archduchess. Wintry sunshine awoke her, shafting across her counterpane, and Marie Louise sat up, rubbing her eyes and yawning before the sudden horror returned. The Monster! Papa still awaited her answer!

She spent the morning riding swiftly, the wind whipping her cheeks and thinking furiously. On her return to her chamber she had had no time to change out of her riding habit when Count Metternich arrived, requesting that she receive him.

'Good morning, Count,' she said graciously, extending her hand for his greeting before seating herself. Bijou pawed her, anxious for a caress. Marie Louise lifted him on to her lap and fondled his ears absently as she awaited the Count's mission in apprehension.

'Your Highness,, your father bids me ask you how you have decided, concerning your future.'

Marie Louise's blue eyes besought his for help. 'How would my father have me decide, Count?'

The Count shook his head. 'His Imperial Majesty charges me to enquire only your desires, not to reveal his own.'

Marie Louise struggled to think. How could she, who had never taken a decision, nay, never been allowed to make a decision in her life, contend with such a fearful problem alone and unaided? Her whole life had been governed by the principles of obedience and submission, and there had been no need for inner debate. How could she now make such a choice, alone?

Obedience and submission, that was the answer still. Her father expected it; Austria had dire need of it. There was no further need of debate. Slowly, painfully, Marie Louise put down the dog, rose from her chair and gazed earnestly out of the window as she answered.

'Count Metternich, pray tell my father that I desire what my duty commands me to desire, when it concerns the interests of the Empire. It is that which one must consider and nothing else. Beg my father only to do his duty as a Sovereign, and not subordinate his will to my personal desires.'

She barely heard Count Metternich's murmured reply. 'Go, Count, go to my father now and tell him I am happy if my sacrifice is not in vain,' she urged him, cutting short his embarrassed acknowledgements. He bowed, and as he left Marie Louise thought she could detect a brightness about his eyes as if tears hovered, before her own brimmed.

That night she heard a coach clattering away and knew the French Ambassador was carrying to Paris the answer for which Bonaparte waited. In another chamber of the Hofburg, the Emperor lay awake. It wasn't his fault, he reflected, that his gentle daughter was obliged to ally herself with the French ruffian. Never before had Austria needed personal sacrifice so desperately. Duty demanded it, and Marie Louise had ever been a dutiful child, and equally it was his duty to sacrifice all that he held dear, even his favourite child, if duty demanded it.

CHAPTER 5

VIENNA, 1810

As in a dream Marie Louise received her first letter from her bridegroom-to-be. The Emperor smiled proudly as she read it aloud.

'My cousin,' the large, unformed hand read, 'The brilliant qualities which distinguish her person have inspired us with the desire to serve and honour her.'

'Hmph!' snorted the Empress. 'I see he presumes to use the royal plural just as if he were truly nobly born.'

'Hush, my dear,' soothed the Emperor. 'Continue, Louise.'

'In begging the Emperor her Father,' Marie Louise's toneless voice continued reading, 'to trust us with the care and happiness of Her Imperial Highness, we hope she shares the feeling which led us to take this step. May we also flatter ourselves that she will not have agreed to it only to fulfil her duty as an obedient daughter.'

The thin voice faltered. 'Is that all?' the Empress demanded.

'No,' admitted Marie Louise. 'He continues.'

'Then read on.'

'If Her Imperial Highness feels inclined towards our person, we can assure her that we shall use every means at our disposal to please her, and to win in the future her entire confidence.'

'No more? That is very abrupt,' remarked Maria Ludovica.

'He ends by saying he hopes I shall regard him most favourably. That is all.'

'There now,' said the Emperor. 'Not so ungracious after all, and it does seem he intends to please you, my dear.'

'That is not surprising when he has had the fortune to win an Emperor's daughter for his bride,' Maria Ludovica commented tartly.

'He does promise a fine wedding,' Francis pointed out. 'He dearly wants it to excel even that of Marie Antionette in pomp and luxury. I understand he is reading up all the papers pertaining to her wedding to make certain our daughter's is even more magnificent. Why, he has even asked for your measurements to be sent to him, my dear, so that he can have a splendid trousseau prepared for you.'

Papa was evidently reconciled to the idea of her going to share the Monster's life, Marie Louise realized sadly. Madame Colloredo, when next she wrote, seemed more concerned for her ex-charge, warning Marie Louise about the unscrupulous Bonaparte family she was about to enter.

'Madame Mère, your future mother-in-law, is a stout-hearted Corsican woman of the soil, stubborn . . . a woman of her country, uneducated but noble in herself, capable of taking up a gun . . . to protect the fruit of her womb.'

Truly, an intimidating mother-in-law with whom to reckon, thought Marie Louise fearfully. And Napoleon's eldest brother, Joseph, sounded no better, 'intelligent, kind, but weak,' wrote Madame. Brother Lucien she declared full of intrigue and rebellious. Jerome, forced by Napoleon to abjure his pretty American wife, now treated his new wife Catherine of Württenberg abominably. Napoleon's sisters Eliza and Pauline Madame dismissed as frivolous and ambitious, but of the sister Caroline she uttered a word of warning.

'Caroline, Queen of Naples, is pretty, full of charm, fascinating, but dangerous—intriguing under the enveloping charm of her personality. So beware!'

Marie Louise felt her already depressed spirits sink lower and lower. How was she, untried and inexperienced, to cope with this nest full of sly, clever creatures as well as trying to bear the Monster's proximity without a shudder? Madame Colloredo's last sentence tried to cheer Marie Louise with a tender touch which she knew would appeal to a sensitive, romantic soul.

'Have no fear, my darling, Napoleon will treat you with the honour due to your exalted rank. Having reached for the stars he will see to it that you are the sun which shines over his Empire.'

The young Archduchess did not doubt that Napoleon would indeed care for her well, but would he love her? She gazed at herself constantly in the mirror, wondering whether her attractions were sufficient to inspire love in a man, especially one reputedly so hard to please as Napoleon Bonaparte.

'He does not even know how I look,' she commented to her lady-in-waiting, Countess Lazanski. 'Suppose he finds me ill-favoured?'

'Nonsense, Your Highness,' the Countess murmured soothingly. 'Such fine fair hair, such rounded, creamy shoulders, a pretty, amiable countenance, and I swear the finest figure I have ever beheld—how could he find you other than highly desirable? He wooed but your name, my dear, and will be entranced to find he obtains a lovely young woman with it.'

'Am I truly pretty, Countess?' Marie Louise asked cautiously. 'But what of my lower lip, thick like all the Hapsburgs?'

'He was wed to Josephine, a Creole with negro blood and the thickest of lips, yet he loved her well.'

Suddenly events began to move swiftly. Napoleon's Counsellor de Floret arrived in Vienna with the marriage contract and details of Napoleon's plans. Marie Louise and he were to be wed in Vienna by proxy, and then the bride conveyed by a route he would decide to Paris. Samples of her shoes and gowns must be sent to him at once so that her trousseau could be prepared. Marie Louise was in a daze. Already it was February, and Bonaparte was proposing that the wedding should take place in early March. By the end of March, only six weeks away, she would be Empress of France, exiled from her home for ever. The thought held infinite terror for Marie Louise, and her only consolation lay in knowing that her fate was sublime, the utter relinquishing of personal happiness for her country's good. The greatest women in history had done no more. From this thought must she draw her comfort.

It was early March and Berthier, Prince de Neuchatel, had arrived in Vienna officially to demand Marie Louise's hand on Napoleon's behalf. In the capital the air resounded to the cries of acclamation and delight, and there was an atmosphere of festival, fine carriages and gold-braided uniforms filling the streets, fireworks and parades, illuminations and cheering crowds. Only Marie Louise, the cynosure of all eyes as she drove to church seated between her parents in an open carriage, could feel none of their joy. She felt bitterly alone, isolated in a fantasy world of sacrifice, like the ancient maiden offered in immolation to the Minotaur. All these festivities, the clash of cymbals and the blare of trumpets, the deluge of scintillating lights and torches, meant nothing to the forlorn girl. In public view she controlled herself stoically, but in the privacy of her chamber she wept.

The day after Berthier's arrival in Vienna he made his official demand of the Archduchess's hand for Napoleon Bonaparte. Arriving in great state at the Hofburg in the evening he was conducted to the Audience Chamber, while Marie Louise waited in an antechamber, trembling and half-hoping her father would yet decide to decline. The voices within rose and fell, barely discernible, but the Emperor's sonorous acceptance was clear.

'I grant my daughter's hand to the Emperor of the French,' he declared, and Marie Louise's heart fell. Now it was irrevocable. Countess Lazanski and Count Edling, her Grand Master, took Marie Louise's elbow on either side of her to remind her that this was the signal for her entrance.

Marie Louise took a deep breath, held her head high, and entered the Chamber with dignity. Advancing to the dais where the father stood, she curtseyed low, made a slight bow to Bertheir, and mounted the dais steps to sit beside her father, her heart fluttering like an agitated bird in a cage. Everyone in the room stood stiffly at attention, the air taut with suspense. Berthier was speaking.

'Madame, your august parents have fulfilled the desires of the Emperor my master,' he said, and went on to speak of political needs being of lesser importance than the Archduchess's happiness, and of the joy of seeing Her Imperial Highness's grace and loveliness united on the same great throne with the genius of power. Marie Louise barely heard him, her mind was in such turmoil. The step was taken, she was betrothed to the Ogre, and they awaited but one word more, her assent, to make the tie indissoluble. She rose slowly.

'The will of my father has ever been mine.' Oh, if only she could quell the tremor in her voice that betrayed her! 'My happiness will ever be his.' With a stubborn effort at self-control, Marie Louise pronounced firmly, 'With my father's permission, I give my consent to my marriage with the Emperor Napoleon.'

A gentle hiss of releasing breaths gave evidence of the relief in the room. Strangely, Marie Louise felt composed now she had spoken, and accepted the letter Berthier offered gracefully.

'From the Emperor, Madame. And also a token of his affection,' Berthier added, beckoning forward an officer of the Grand Embassy. The officer advanced stiffly, bearing a velvet cushion on which lay a miniature portrait of Napoleon. Marie Louise heard Countess Lazanski's gasp of delight on beholding it, an exquisite miniature surrounded by sixteen huge diamonds and attached to a fine gold chain.

'If His Imperial Majesty will permit. . . ?' She raised her eyes dutifully to her father. He nodded eagerly, and Countess Lazanski's fingers were quick to seize the portrait. In moments it lay on Marie Louise's breast. Berthier was making an enthusiastic, flattering speech to the Empress Maria Ludovica who, in her turn, smiled and spoke equally insincere words of welcome. Marie Louise could not help a feeling of shame that under this veneer of courteous behaviour so much hatred and scorn of her future husband lay hidden. She kept silent, fingering the portrait thoughtfully, until the Audience was at an end and she could return to the sanctuary of her own room.

A knock came. Prince Berthier was announced, and he strode quickly in. Marie Louise brushed away her tears, ashamed lest they be seen, but Berthier's quick eyes had noticed them. The Archduchess stared miserably at this man who was the emissary of her fate, unable to control her dislike for his clumsy build, his head over-large for his body and his big, red hands with the fingernails bitten right down to the quick. Even in his brilliant gold uniform he was not impressive, slouching and ill at ease. He bowed low.

'Your Highness, forgive my intrusion,' he said uncomfortably. 'I came only to inform you of the details of the proxy wedding, but I fear I have come upon you at a nostalgic moment. I shall retire and return later, if you wish it.'

Marie Louise's dislike faded. He was observant and courteous despite his gross appearance, and she felt explanation was due to him for her silence.

'I am sorry, Prince Berthier. You are right, I was regretting the loss of all my treasures.' Her slim hand waved gracefully, indicating the sketches, water-colours on the tapestried walls, the trinkets and ornaments on shelves and tables. "All these things are souvenirs of happier days, and I am loth to leave them. I am very fond of my boudoir, and was but taking sentimental leave of them. Forgive a foolish girl's emotion.'

Berthier's bright eyes grew gentle. 'Then Madame I will not intrude on such a private moment. Pray forgive my unwarranted discourtesy, and I hope I may have leave to speak with you later.'

Gracefully he withdrew, and Marie Louise was grateful for his sympathetic understanding. Her pet dog whimpered at her feet, and Marie Louise gathered him up lovingly.

'And you, my little Bijou, you most of all I shall weep to lose.' As Countess Lazanski bustled in at this moment, the Archduchess rose, putting the dog aside and crossing to sit at her dressing table. The Countess began brushing her hair. Marie Louise opened her inlaid jewel casket and regarded its contents with a wry smile.

'I had never thought much of jewellery,' she commented quietly, 'but this seems scarcely riches for a future Empress. See, I have but a coral necklace, a brooch of seed pearls and a few hair rings. Do you think Bonaparte will think me an impoverished bride?'

The Countess chuckled. 'Not he, Your Highness, he counts himself lucky enough to have a bride of royal birth. And with all his wealth he will soon provide all the jewels you have ever dreamt of.'

'I dream of none, Countess. It is the simple things that give me contentment—warmth and love, appreciation and my own little treasures.' Tears hovered on Marie Louise's long-fringed lashes, but she brushed them away sternly. This was no time for self-pity; pity enough glowed in the eyes of the populace and the courtiers who regarded her in awe and wonder.

Two days of festivities followed, banquets and operas and pyrotechnic displays and parades such as the impoverished Court could afford, and the mundane business affairs of Marie Louise's wedding were disposed of, the relinquishing of her claim to the Austrian throne, the payment of her dowry of half a million francs, and the signing of the marriage contract. Throughout these events Marie Louise allowed herself to be led, magnificently costumed in tulle and brocade, feeling herself to be no more than a pretty puppet.

Lent was approaching. The marriage must be concluded swiftly. On March 11th, 1810, Marie Louise drove the few yards from the Hofburg to the adjacent Church of the Capucins to be married, but so befuddled were her wits that she had only a hazy impression of brilliant candlelight and gems, plumes and sabres and tapestries and the figure of her uncle, Archduke Charles, who was her proxy bridegroom, kneeling beside her on a prie-dieu. She remembered making the correct response—'I will and so promise'—when the Archbishop asked her if she would take to husband the illustrious Napoleon Bonaparte, and the exchanging of rings, but little more, for her already confused mind was further confounded by a sudden pealing of bells and booming of gun salutes.

Guests thronged the church, crushed in the galleries and outside in the square, dazzlingly colourful and spectacular. Marie Louise was overwhelmed with pressing congratulations and good wishes, and watched the French embassy officials, her new subjects, kneel before her in obeisance. At the State banquet which followed, carried out in accordance with Napoleon's instructions, she sat at the centre of a horseshoe-shaped table, her parents at either hand. The Emperor smiled at her weakly, inclining his head to whisper to her.

'You are Empress of France now, Luischen.'

'I can scarcely believe it, Papa.'

'And do you realize also that, as you are the wife of our conqueror, we are but your vassals now, daughter?'

Marie Louise gazed at him, horrified. 'Oh, no, Papa!'

He smiled again, wryly. 'It is true. I hope that through your graces our son-in-law will think kindly of us and treat us well.'

Marie Louise made no answer. Only now was the great and terrible importance of her role becoming clear to her. She looked at her stepmother, chatting brightly to Berthier, and saw that the French Ambassador's thoughtful gaze was resting on her.

'I shall do what I must, Papa, do not fear. You shall come to no harm through me,' she murmured, and for a second her father's hand covered hers beneath the table.

Next morning Berthier and his embassy officials drove away, amid cheering crowds, to return with news of the proxy wedding to Napoleon, leaving their new Empress to follow shortly with Countess Lazanski. Marie Louise, left with forty thousand francs as a gift from Napoleon, debated what to do with the money.

'No Countess, I shall not buy jewels,' she told the eager Countess Lazanski. 'I shall distribute it instead among our noble wounded who fought so valiantly but in vain to protect us from the French.'

And that same afternoon, the last day she was to spend in her native country, Marie Louise drove out to tour the hospitals. The soldiers hailed her with pleasure, paying homage to the noble maid who was to ransom their country, but all Marie Louise could remember as she drove back to the Hofburg was the wistful look of pity in their eyes.

CHAPTER 6

PARIS, 1810

QUEEN CAROLINE of Naples reclined gracefully on a chaise longue in the Tuileries, yawning and stretching her voluptuous figure with sensuous feline grace. She watched her brother Napoleon who stood, silent and brooding, by the inlaid desk cluttered with maps and despatches, and thought for the thousandth time how strange it was that such a man could hold half Europe, trembling, in the palm of his hand.

True, he held all the Bonapartes in his thrall too—Lucien, Louis, Joseph, Jerome, Pauline, Caroline herself—none of them dared defy his iron determination, born of the same stubborn blood though they were. Like Madame Mère, their grizzled old mother who made no secret of the fact that she adored Napoleon best of all her brood, they were all equally ambitious and scheming, Caroline no less than the others, but it was curious why Napoleon above all should be the one to dominate. After all, she thought, just look at him, short of figure and squat of limb, his overlarge head disproportionate to his short frame and his face stubbornly set—what was there about Napoleon to set him above and apart from the rest of the numerous Bonaparte progeny?

Whatever it was, she admitted reluctantly to herself, she respected and loved this sombre, moody brother of hers, and he exacted respect if nothing else from all who encountered him. Until lately, that was, because now he was behaving like an over-excited schoolboy anticipating a fabulous gift, so feverish and animated he was over this Austrian chit, Marie Louise who, by all accounts, was as dull and unexciting as German women usually were.

Napoleon turned from the desk, stroking his chin thoughtfully.

'So, Caroline, I have decided to send you to meet my bride at Braunau,' he said, and Caroline remembered he had been talking of the arrangements for Marie Louise's reception just before he relapsed into one of his unaccountable silences.

'Ah yes, you were saying," she replied smoothly. 'At the border just as Marie Antoinette was received there. And you, like King Louis, I presume, will await your bride at Compiègne?'

'Of course.'

Of course he would. Just as he had made sure to mimic that other royal wedding in every way, improving upon it even in magnificence where he could. Just as he had ordered her to prepare the most impressive trousseau any bride had ever seen. Caroline felt envy gnawing.

'Really, Napoleon, such extravagance over her trousseau! I had nothing like that when I married Murat. Do you truly think any girl can use a hundred and forty-four chemises and eighty nightcaps? And as for two gross of handkerchieves, well! You must be expecting your bride to be very unhappy!'

Napoleon shrugged, dismissing her comment as of no account. Caroline refrained from remarking that he had never made a gift to *her* of such elegant cashmere shawls, such hunting-habits and gowns, and those marvellous little satin and velvet boots, embroidered and fringed and embellished with grebe and ermine. Even insignificant items like garters and combs and fans were jewelled and monogrammed, and every one had been subjected to his critical scrutiny.

Silver-gilt dressing cases, gilded chamber-pots and even toothpicks of solid gold—was there no end to the extravagance he would lavish on this creature? Napoleon was fidgeting with the red morocco portfolios on his desk.

'Do you think my messengers were honest, Caroline, when they told me the girl is fair?'

Caroline shrugged indolently. 'They say she is agreeable of countenance, save for the Hapsburg lip, slim, but with a fine bust and bottom—what more can you want of a girl you are marrying for her lineage, not her looks?'

'They say she is gentle and innocent, unused to the ways of the world, having been brought up in seclusion,' he commented reflectively.

'The more docile, the easier to train to your ways.'

'She seems intelligent enough, from what they tell me. She speaks several languages.'

'Including French, mercifully.' Caroline's laughter rippled through the great chamber, and she saw her brother's dour expression relax.

'Yes, thank God.'

Caroline smiled wickedly. 'You, thank God, brother? You, who hold his vicar the Pope imprisoned in Savone? Many would think you mocked at religion to speak thus.'

'That is enough.' Napoleon's voice cracked whip-like into Caroline's pleasant, teasing speech, causing her to turn pale. She knew well that emphatic tone, and knew she had gone too far.

'Now listen to me,' he continued, his voice staccato and businesslike, but his scowling brows denoting the anger he felt at being thus touched on the raw. 'You will travel to Braunau to meet Marie Louise. On the journey home you will endeavour to reassure her, to convince her I am not the monster she undoubtedly believes I am. By the time you reach

Compiègne and me, I trust you will so have won her confidence that she will believe you.'

'Yes, Napoleon.' Caroline's voice was meek, but inwardly she was plotting. Indeed, she would do all in her power to win the girl over, as Napoleon asked, for through Marie Louise Caroline could gain from Napoleon advantages for herself and Murat. If the girl was as docile as they said, she should be malleable clay indeed for a shrewd and devious Bonaparte like herself.

'Now leave me, and send Bourrienne to me,' Napoleon ordered tersely. Caroline rose leisurely and walked gracefully to the door, where she turned.

'Should I arrange dancing lessons for you, Napoleon?' she asked sweetly. 'A girl of eighteen is bound to love dancing, and she might consider you an old man indeed, to be forty and never dance.'

There was laughter in her lovely eyes, for she meant it only as sisterly teasing, but to her surprise Napoleon nodded briskly. 'That is true. Please arrange the lessons. Now leave me to work with Bourrienne.'

And Caroline, mildly surprised, bade him goodnight and left, knowing that poring over his maps and dispatches he would become oblivious of time and probably keep his poor, overworked secretary awake, blinking and red-eyed, until dawn. He would brood no longer on Marie Louise's appearance for, knowing she came of fertile stock, being one of thirteen children and her mother one of over twenty, the chances were very high that she would give him what he craved most—a son.

Meanwhile, the object of all Napoleon's plans was making the painful severance from her family in order to set out on the journey to a new life fraught with fear. As Marie Louise's coach rumbled on through the grey mist of rain, taking her further and further from Vienna and her beloved family, her tears fell freely as she recalled the parting.

'Have courage, Luischen,' the Crown Prince Ferdi had said firmly, but his pale face and wide eyes had worried Marie Louise. Maybe the shock of parting would bring on another of his fits, for he was a delicate youth. Leopoldine's pretty face had been made red and ugly with tears as Marie Louise shared out her few jewels with her sisters.

'I shall miss you,' Luischen,' she had wept.

'Perhaps one day soon you too will marry a great king and set out on an adventure of your own,' Marie Louise had commented gaily, in an effort to reassure her.

'Make the most of your opportunities, child,' the Empress had exhorted, and her face alone had remained smiling and tearfree. Papa's lip was trembling. Marie Louise had squeezed him close, unable to speak for the lump which clogged her throat.

'Do whatever your husband bids you,' Papa muttered, his voice husky with emotion. 'Remember that, Luischen, do absolutely anything he tells you.' Blinded by tears, Marie Louise simply nodded.

Countess Lazanski, seated opposite Marie Louise in the gilded coach, gazed out over the rain-soaked fields, her eyes remote and dreamy. Already she was visualizing life in the Tuileries Palace and revelling in the glory to come, Marie Louise thought sadly, for Paris held no terror of an Ogre for her.

What manner of husband would he be, this tyrant of Europe? They said he was short and ugly and fiery-tempered, yet he had sworn he intended to please and content her. But how could a man who had been the terror of her life, twice driving her from home into exile, now hope to love as a husband should?

'Countess,' Marie Louise murmured, watching the other woman start as her voice recalled her to the present, 'do you know what today is?'

'No, Your Majesty?'

'It is Tuesday, March 13th. The thirteenth, mark you. It is an evil omen.'

'Not so, I am sure. That is but idle superstition.'

'You may be right, Countess. It is true I did not see the White Lady as I expected. She always came before when there was trouble to come. I can but hope her non-appearance was a happy portent.'

'I am certain of it. You will be happy, I know, once you come to know and love your husband.'

Marie Louise sighed. Countess Lazanski was a romantic, optimistic soul, but surely even she was hoping for too much that anyone could love a creature such as this Napoleon Bonaparte.

Suddenly the coach clattered to a halt. It was at Saint Poiten, where they were to stay for the night before driving on in the morning to the frontier, where Queen Caroline awaited them at Braunau. Wearily Marie Louise dismounted and made for the door of the little inn. A figure stood silhouetted in the doorway against the lamplight within.

'Luischen!' a voice croaked, hoarse with emotion. With a surge of delight Marie Louise recognized her father, and flung herself joyfully into his arms.

'I could not let you go away, perhaps for ever, without a final glimpse of your beloved face,' he murmured. Marie Louise clasped him closer, sobbing with joy mingled with grief. 'I shall travel with you as far as Ems, if you will permit.' She nodded eagerly.

The next day the harrowing scene of parting took place all over again. In the coach, alone with Countess Lazanski once more, Marie Louise felt sick and dizzy. As if her tribulations were not enough, from the cold rainy weather and the draughty coach and inn she had caught cold.

The horses were wading ankle-deep in mud; passing peasants stared, bedraggled and curious, at the coach and rainsodden guards. Occasionally Marie Louise would rub clear a patch on the misted windows and survey the desolate scene outside, the shattered, devastated villages and fields laid waste by the Monster only—how long ago?—only ten months earlier.

The second night's stop was at Ried. The next morning, according to Napoleon's instructions, Marie Louise was to drive to Braunau and there the official handing-over of the Empress of the French was to take place after lunch. Marie Louise arrived in the dreary little garrison town, shivering with cold and sneezing. Without delay she was stripped of her travelling costume and arrayed in a court gown of gold brocade, heavy with encrusted embroidery. Countess Lazanski's fingers were as icy as Marie Louise's heart as they deftly pinned, and fastened at last the portrait of Napoleon about Marie Louise's neck.

'Take heart, my child,' the Countess murmured as they were then led to the garrison. A building had there been erected consisting of three pavilions lying immediately on the border, one pavilion representing Austria, one France, and the one between neutral territory. Marie Louise was led into the west wing. 'What now?' she enquired timidly of Prince Trautmannsdorff, who was charged with handing her over to France.

'In a moment we move into the neutral wing where the French delegation awaits. After the official ceremony you will pass on to the French wing, and the French have received their new Empress.'

It was time. Marie Louise threw back her head proudly and followed Prince Trautmannsdorff into the adjacent pavilion, taking her place upon the throne which stood upon a dais. From the further side a number of French people appeared, and Marie Louise smiled to recognize Prince Berthier. He advanced, bowed three times, and then carried out the official announcement and exchange of papers with Prince Trautmannsdorff. It was tedious, all this speechmaking, first in French and then in German, then the signing, but at last it was done.

The double doors to the French wing were thrown wide. Marie Louise walked through without a backward glance, Countess Lazanski following. Now it was complete—she was the French Empress on French soil. Already Berthier was presenting her new household to her.

'Her Majesty Queen Caroline of Naples,' he announced, and a young, voluptuous woman of dark, dramatic beauty flung her arms cordially about the new Empress. Marie Louise, unaccustomed to such intimacy, felt herself stiffen. It was unaccountable really, for the young woman with the warm smile and a glittering crown seemed truly anxious to be friendly. Other ladies crowded round, peacock-fine in their gorgeous gowns compared to the stately, less elaborate Viennese ladies, but Marie Louise paid them little attention as she studied the beautiful Caroline and wondered at her own unease.

'Come,' said Caroline at last, drawing her by the elbow, 'there is time enough to become acquainted with your new ladies of the household. Let me show you the trousseau my brother has prepared for you.'

She drew Marie Louise further into the French pavilion, ignoring Countess Lazanski who followed. Marie Louise's eyes grew round. Not only was the French pavilion far more elegant and ornate than the Austrian one, but the gifts now heaped on her from Napoleon were breathtaking. A magnificent silver-gilt dressing set . . . gold and jewels beyond price . . . and the most overwhelming gowns and chemises she had ever seen.

'My brother the Emperor is most anxious that you should become French at once,' Caroline was murmuring sweetly, starting to unfasten Marie Louise's bodice. 'He insists that you wear all French clothes from the moment of your arrival, so let us strip you of this cumbersome gold thing and re-dress you according to our ways.'

Protesting, Marie Louise was divested not only of her gown but of her chemise and all her underthings. Caroline smiled in amusement to see Marie Louise's shocked expression.

'You are not prudish, sister, surely?' she mocked. Marie Louise felt her dislike grow. It was enough that this coarse creature laughed at her, but to call her sister on such short acquaintance was immensely distasteful. It was difficult, however, to stand on one's dignity when revealed, stark-naked, to an amused circle of ladies. Only Countess Lazanski's reddened face betrayed sympathy.

For two hours those intrusive fingers dressed and scented, brushed and coiled. At last they were content, and Marie Louise regarded herself in surprise in the long cheval glass. They had done well, beautifying her as no one had ever done before, but she felt strange and unfamiliar in these unaccustomed clothes, her bodice cut so low that her full breasts had difficulty in remaining concealed. And the perfume was overpowering.

At the banquet which followed Marie Louise was well aware of the tension. The French, including Caroline, were doing their best to be hearty and convivial but the Austrians remained stiff and unbending. They too resented the handing

c

over of their princess to their conqueror, and the obvious way
in which the French had taken possession of her and made
her over.

'Will you take my father a letter on your return to reassure
him I am well?' she whispered to Prince Trautmannsdorff during the meal.

'To be sure.'

So late that night Marie Louise's quill scratched on convulsively by candlelight, thoughts pouring from her pen.
Beloved Papa must be reassured she was content.

> 'I am thinking of you and will continue to do so. . . .
> Almighty God has given me the strength to support this
> last painful shock, the separation from my loved ones. . . .
> I shall find consolation in the knowledge that I have done
> my duty in making this sacrifice. . . .'

Swiftly, sketchy paragraphs outlined her arrival at
Braunau and the official ceremony, then a mention of the
agony of parting from her ladies. Marie Louise could not
resist a comment about Caroline.

> 'The Queen of Naples was the first to come and meet
> me. . . . I embraced her and was wonderfully polite, but I
> do not trust her for one moment. I think her zeal is not
> the only motive for her journey.'

She reported then on Napoleon's gifts and the impressive
trousseau, but at the end could not resist a cry.

> 'Oh, how deep is my regret not to be able to be with
> you, my beloved Papa!'

Next day the journey continued, Caroline and Countess
Lazanski sharing Marie Louise's coach. That night they
were received at a banquet given by the King and Queen of

Bavaria in Munich. Despite her magnificence, clothed in Napoleon's breathtaking gowns and jewels, Marie Louise was still uneasy. Caroline had a furtive, cunning look about her whenever she looked at Countess Lazanski, and Marie Louise feared her power.

'Nonsense,' said the Countess as she laid out Marie Louise's nightgown. 'I fear you are obsessed with your own vulnerability, my dear. No one would dream of taking me from you, the only friend you have left.'

But as if decreed by fate, Prince Berthier presented himself at that moment. Within moments he had left, and Marie Louise sat, stunned and miserable, on the edge of her bed. Napoleon had decreed that Lazanski must return to Austria, and only French ladies were to serve his Empress!

'It is *her* doing, I know it!' Marie Louise wept bitterly. 'I shall never forgive her for this.'

'Prince Berthier says it is the Emperor's order,' the weeping Countess pointed out.

'No, no! It is not by his order, I am certain; but her I shall never trust again.'

Heartbroken, she wrote again to her father.

'I could make my husband no greater sacrifice,' she wrote, 'although I am certain the idea was not his.'

But if by her action Caroline intended to come closer to her, to wield some power over her, Marie Louise decided firmly, her attempt was doomed to failure. Who was this parvenu upstart, this Queen with a crown usurped from Marie Louise's own grandmother on her head, to presume intimacy with *her*?

Caroline seemed imperturable. Sunnily she chatted as the coach rumbled on towards Compiègne and Napoleon, and Marie Louise took secret delight in having cheated the devious Queen. Banned though Countess Lazanski was from Marie Louise's sight, she had succeeded in sneaking into Marie Louise's chamber for a final, tearful farewell before Marie Louise continued her journey to a new life. Defiantly she refused to enthuse when Caroline drew her attention to the five splendid white horses Napoleon had supplied to draw her coach. Stubbornly she declined to acknowledge the crowds who cried 'Long Live the Empress' as she and her nineteen other carriages containing her officials and equerries clattered by. Caroline sat eyeing her quizzically.

'I hope you mean to try as hard to please Napoleon as he is endeavouring to please you,' she commented tartly.

'Please him?' echoed Marie Louise. 'What does he wish of me, may I ask?'

'Only that you be fertile and produce him sons to inherit his acquisitions,' Caroline replied coolly. 'To one of your build and prolific family that should not be too difficult. Give him a son and then you may ask of my brother whatever you will.'

Marie Louise sat silent. The coach was rumbling on to where her husband waited, not so very many miles away, and suddenly it occurred to the new Empress that in her anxiety over marrying the Ogre she had overlooked one point. Lacking a mother of her own, she had meant to ask Maria Ludovica to tell her just how babies were begotten. She knew only that it was as a result of some kind of ritual between man and wife—kissing full on the lips, Victoire had once confided giggling, in the darkness of the huge bed—but surely, amongst all the other commands she had received as to her behaviour towards Napoleon, they should have told her this important part. Her anguish must have shown in her face, for Caroline leaned forward inquisitively.

'What is it, Marie Louise? You look very pale all of a sudden.'

'It is nothing—this cold, perhaps.' Marie Louise sat biting her lip, perplexed and worried. Perhaps after all it would be as well to confide her ignorance to Caroline who, after all, was married and would know the secret. Trying hard to appear cool, Marie Louise asked her diffidently.

Caroline's face was a picture of amazement. 'Do you truly mean you have been sent here in complete ignorance? Did no one instruct you?'

'My mother is dead,' Marie Louise answered quietly. 'My stepmother and I were never—close. Pray you do me the service of instructing me in all I should know.'

Caroline cocked her dark head to one side, surveying Marie Louise thoughtfully. 'In truth,' she said at length, perhaps the Emperor would prefer to instruct you himself, so that you learn only the ways that please him. It would be intrusive of me to forestall him.'

'Please!' Marie Louise could not repress the pleading in her voice. Countess Lazanski would have told her all, but in the absence of friends even Caroline could be helpful. Enlightenment as to this strange ritual was all she wanted.

The coach slowed, lurching in the mud-rutted lane.

'We must have reached Courcelles, where we are to stay,' remarked Caroline. 'Yes, I can see the lights of the château.'

Suddenly the coach door sprang open, and without waiting to lower the folded steps, a uniformed, mud-spattered figure leapt in. His eyes gleamed ferociously, his short hair clung damply to his brow, and his hands reached out for Marie Louise.

'Brigands!' she shrieked in alarm.

'Napoleon!' cried Caroline.

CHAPTER 7

FRANCE, 1810

MARIE LOUISE sat frozen, rendered immobile by shock and disbelief. This man, this short creature with a thickening body clothed in the uniform of a guard, was he the man she had dreaded meeting? Swiftly he bent, his rainsodden cloak enveloping her too, and he kissed her soundly on the cheek.

Caroline stared, startled. 'Napoleon! I did not expect to see you until Compiègne! What brings you here, brother?'

Napoleon answered, his eyes raking Marie Louise with feverish curiosity. 'I could not wait, sister. I was burning with desire to see my bride. Murat rode with me. Go you to your husband—he is at the château—and leave me a while.'

Caroline murmured some words of apology and disappeared through the still-open door through which the rain was dashing. Napoleon closed it after her and seated himself, smiling broadly, beside Marie Louise. Taking her hands in his he scanned her face closely.

'You are indeed pretty, ma bonne Louise," he murmured. Marie Louise, still dazed, stared at his face blankly. He was not handsome, this upstart Emperor, but there was a classical air about his fine head, reminiscent of a Greek god. He was pale and there was a sadness about him despite his smile, as though he were by nature a melancholy and contemplative man. And those eyes. . . . Napoleon's gaze was frank and searching, compelling honesty from Marie Louise's honest soul.

'Your—your portrait does not do you justice, sir.' She was fingering the miniature about her neck. Napoleon removed her fingers and bent to kiss her neck, and Marie Louise felt a flush redden her cheeks.

She was conscious of her hair falling awry, the curls escaping like unruly tendrils, and wished she had been better prepared. But he seemed not to notice; on the contrary he seemed highly delighted.

'Nor did my messengers paint you in your full beauty, Louise,' he murmured. You are entrancing.' Flinging aside his sodden cloak, he sat again close by her, easing back her red fur-lined wrap the better to behold her. Marie Louise felt shame redden her cheeks. Like a farmer he was examining the prize heifer he had bought, she thought, but his probing fingertips on her neck and shoulders aroused a pleasurable sensation nevertheless. She watched the slender fingers, fascinated. This was the hand that had wielded the sabre against her countrymen at Marengo and Austerlitz. This low, resonant voice murmuring praise and endearments was the same that thundered orders to attack her compatriots—and also to spare her in her illness, she remembered charitably, recalling how he had left her in peace in the Hofburg when he took Vienna.

The tingling sensation caused by his gentle hand and his lips so close to her ear gave rise to other thoughts. Those hands had caressed other women—the Polish countess Marie Walewska that time in Schönbrunn, and not so long ago the unfortunate Josephine. It was odd to think that it was barely three months since he had divorced the sensuous, attractive Creole who, if report be true, was Napoleon's only real love. How could she, a mere girl of eighteen, unversed in the ways of men, hope to compete with the exotic Josephine? If Napoleon had married Marie Louise only for political reasons, would it ever be possible for her to drive all thoughts of his former passionate wife from his mind?

Suddenly Napoleon leapt to the door and leaned out, bawling orders into the night. Onwards to Compiègne, he commanded, forget the arrangements. Let the coaches rattle on swiftly through the night to where his court awaited him in the château at Compiègne. By the time they arrived there, rain was still falling.

'Come, Louise, let us go into the château.' Napoleon's voice, though gentle, was blurred with a timbre Marie Louise had never heard in a man's voice and it caused a strange sensation within her she had never before experienced. His eyes, dark and brooding, were half-closed, but the look beneath the veiling lids was as fierce and penetrating as ever. His mouth came down gently on hers, a kiss light and chaste, and Marie Louise shuddered in emotion. He rose abruptly.

'Come,' he said, drawing her cloak about her, then flinging his own cloak over them both, he led her swiftly through the rain. Caroline stood at the top of the steps, a tall, handsome man beside her.

'Napoleon,' she said tentatively, laying a hand on his sleeve.

'What is it?' he demanded brusquely. 'It is late, and time we were all abed. I am sure Murat agrees.'

Marie Louise passed the huddled figures, into the shelter of the hall, but Caroline's whispered words came to her ears nonetheless.

'Your retinue awaits you, Napoleon, and the rest of the family are eager to see your bride—Jerome, Pauline, Hortense and all the others.'

'Bid them go to bed. They shall meet her tomorrow. For now, it is bed for us all.'

'Do you mean to sleep with your bride tonight, Napoleon?'

'Why not? We are officially wed, though the civil ceremony

has not yet been held. Do you dispute I have the right?' His voice, though low, was ringing clear.

'No, brother. Only—take care with her. She is totally ignorant. Do not affright her; it would pay you well to be gentle with her.'

A snort accompanied Napoleon's clattering footsteps as he rejoined Marie Louise and led her up the staircase. At the head of the stairs he paused, taking Marie Louise by the shoulders and gazing at her with smouldering, intent eyes.

'Louise, are you afraid of me?'

'I—I think not.'

'Do you perhaps like me—a little?'

'A little, yes. And as I come to know you, no doubt I shall like you better still.'

'You shall, Louise, I promise. Only remember your destiny, my dear, as Empress of France. There will be many functions you will dislike, perhaps, but you must always appear serene and indefatigable. It will be hard, but have no fear. I shall always be with you, loving and concerned for you. Remember that.'

'Yes, Napoleon.'

'You do not then disapprove if I take you to wife tonight? Must we wait until the civil marriage service is performed?'

Marie Louise hung her head. Unaccustomed to making decisions of her own, she could only murmur, 'My father bade me obey you in all things, Napoleon.'

'Then that is settled,' he declared in satisfaction. 'And when our son is born, we shall be secure and happy.'

His son! Marie Louise remembered then with a shock that it was to be her prime duty to provide Napoleon with an heir. But she had no idea where to begin!

Taking the hand he held out to her, she followed him resignedly into the chamber. Obey, Father had said.

In the morning Caroline was disappointed that Napoleon and Marie Louise did not appear at breakfast, preferring to eat in the privacy of their own room. It was nearing mid-day before Napoleon emerged, still in his dressing gown and his dark face sparkling with good humour.

'Oh, German girls!' he enthused, patting Caroline's shoulder contentedly as he passed. 'They make the best wives in the world, sweet, good, simple, and as fresh as roses!'

Caroline smiled wryly. So Marie Louise had contented Napoleon it seemed. Evidently his tactics had been not half so ruthless in bed as on the battlefield if, as it appeared, he had elicited the response he craved from her. And when, late in the afternoon, Marie Louise eventually emerged she wore the dreamy, languorous expression of a woman newly-awakened to the delights of the marriage bed. A sudden transformation, Caroline mused, from the innocent girl of yesterday. Napoleon had wasted no time in attempting to beget his son.

Marie Louise was floating on a cloud of happiness. No one had even ventured to suggest to her that the ritual she had dreaded could be so exciting. Marriage was indeed a pleasant state. How tenderly Napoleon cared for her, even to providing the most magnificent bathroom! She recalled how she had revelled in the warm, scented waters of the bath in its octagonal room, the walls gleaming with white taffeta and East Indian shawls, and how she had averted her eyes demurely from the nude figures painted on the panels.

'Did you sleep well?' Caroline asked mockingly when Marie Louise joined the others. Murrat choked on his cup of chocolate.

'Thank you, I am much refreshed,' answered Marie Louise, and wondered at Caroline's amused laughter.

Before dinner there was music, a beautiful Italian soprano

named Grassini singing to the accompaniment of a German composer named Paer. Marie Louise closed her eyes and listened to the soaring notes enraptured, conscious that in her pink gown and with heightened colour in her cheeks she looked her prettiest. The night's events had given her confidence, and she no longer feared the awesome array of Napoleon's family.

There was his brother, Louis, King of Holland, looking immensely bored with the music. He had a sour, brooding face and limped somewhat, as if rheumaticky. He looked far too preoccupied with himself and his miseries to take much notice of his friendly-faced wife, Hortense, who sat beside him. Marie Louise regarded her curiously, the daughter of the woman she had supplanted and wondered how Hortense regarded her.

Napoleon's youngest sister, Pauline, was by far the prettiest, Marie Louise decided; dainty and small-boned, she looked like some ethereal creature from a fairytale as she sat tapping her toe to the beat of the music. And judging by the way in which all eyes lingered on her loveliness, many of the men present in the room thought so too.

Jerome, King of Westphalia sat proudly, resplendent in his brocaded uniform, next to his plump, haughty wife, Catherine of Württemberg. Marie Louise found herself eyeing Catherine curiously, a bride who, like herself, had been obliged to marry a Bonaparte and who, from the adoring looks she occasionally cast his way, had had no reason to regret the marriage.

Nobility everywhere. Over there sat the fat, gouty Russian ambassador, Prince Kurakin, and next to him the puny Prince de Frias, representing Joseph King of Spain. Nearby the Prince of Baden, escorting his dainty wife Princess Stephanie, glowered at Archduke Ferdinand, Marie Louise's uncle.

An impressive collection, the new Empress mused, and felt sure they would all forgive her shyness and reserve, for it was not easy to be amiable with so many strangers, and in French too. Was Napoleon satisfied with her behaviour so far? She glanced sideways at her bridegroom, and saw to her dismay that he was nodding, eyes closed, and obviously asleep.

Marie Louise looked up, caught Caroline's amused smile, and blushed. They were no doubt thinking, all of them, that his night-time exertions had exhausted him. She nudged him gently in the ribs.

'Yes? What is it?' he demanded sharply, alert at once.

'You were sleeping, Napoleon. I feared you might snore.'

'I never snore. I have a facility for falling asleep anywhere, any time, even on my feet if I need sleep.'

'I am sorry I disturbed you.'

His set expression dissolved at once into a smile. 'Not at all, Louise, it is I who should apologise. Such discourtesy to a ravishing bride! Now I promise I shall stay awake, if only to enjoy looking at you.'

Marie Louise dimpled graciously. Napoleon, leaning forward, took her hand. 'Indeed, I think I shall write to your father this very night, telling him how you fulfil all my hopes, and assuring him again that I shall make you happy.'

Another night of bliss for Marie Louise in the château of Compiègne followed, and even by day her devoted husband could not tear himself from her side. His secretary's reproachful glances that the dossiers and portfolios in the Emperor's cabinet lay forgotten, went unheeded.

'Tomorrow, mignonne," murmured Napoleon as they lay contentedly that night, 'tomorrow we drive to St. Cloud for our civil ceremony. Then, two days later, we shall have our grand church wedding in the Tuileries, and there will be the

Senators and Marshals and Counsellors of State and the Cardinals to witness our union. Then, my love, we shall be indissolubly one.'

In the morning, before their departure, Marie Louise wrote happily to her father : 'I am constantly with him, he loves me profoundly, and I return his affection. I am sure I shall live happy with him.'

At St. Cloud a vast assembly of dignitaries awaited their new Empress, and Marie Louise felt like a dazed puppet manipulated by her solicitous master as Napoleon led her gently by the hand through the throng and into the castle. That night they slept restlessly, for after a storm of their own making the elements provided the bridal pair with yet another, thunder crashing and rain pelting heavily throughout the night. By dawn, the day of their nuptials, the rain still fell mercilessly.

Hundred of guests crowded the scarlet and black gallery to watch Marie Louise and Napoleon mount the two Imperial thrones raised upon a dais under a golden canopy. Marie Louise looked at Napoleon in rapture; in his magnificent flame-coloured cloak he looked superb, and she could see his eyes registering satisfaction at her appearance. The mirror had already told her she looked well; her chestnut-gilt hair and blue eyes taking on a fresh radiance enhanced as they were by the splendid silver court gown, the circlet of jewel-encrusted gold on her forehead and the blaze of emeralds about her throat.

Rain still spattered angrily at the window panes that evening as they sat down to the wedding banquet, and Marie Louise could hear the muttered gloom of the guests.

'It does not augur well, this foul weather,' they murmured between sips of wine. 'It is an evil omen for the wedding.'

Napoleon was smiling contentedly, unaware of the unease

until Cardinal Fesch made his way to the Emperor's side to whisper confidentially. Marie Louise saw Napoleon's smile fade instantly, to be replaced by a look of pure anger.

'Will they so?' he roared, leaping to his feet so furiously that his silver goblet clattered to his feet, spilling its contents in an unheeded pool. 'What is it, Napoleon?' Marie Louise cried in alarm, clutching at his sleeve. It was his sudden fury as well as the cause of it that frightened her.

'The Cardinals—half of them dare to question my divorce. The insolence! To question the validity of our union!'

Cardinal Fesch murmured soothing words that Marie Louise could not catch. Napoleon sat down again slowly, shrugging his shoulders.

'Abstain from attending the religious ceremony, will they? Bah, they do not dare!' So saying, he took Marie Louise's hand again with a smile, dismissing Cardinal Fesch and his unwelcome rumour.

But when, towards dawn, Marie Louise awoke from a deep slumber, Napoleon was not beside her. Sitting up with a start, she saw his figure silhouetted against the window. Rain was still lashing fiercely against the panes. He came back to the bedside.

'You were sleeping so peacefully. You look angelic when you are asleep,' he murmured. 'I could not sleep. Do you hear the sound outside? It is the footsteps of our faithful subjects, entering the city to watch our wedding, Despite the fearful rain they come, anxious to share my joy and drink to our health in the wine which will flow in the fountains.'

Marie Louise was touched by his words. Whatever was disturbing Napoleon, he was endeavouring to reassure her. Was it the Cardinals' revolt which worried him, or the evil augury of the tempestuous weather? Hardly the latter, she thought. Napoleon was too powerful a man, too confident of his ability to be made fearful by primitive superstitution. She looked at him fondly, paler than ever in the half-light of dawn, and admired once again the strength of his countenance. He was staring out of the window again, deep in thought, and it crossed Marie Louise's mind that his air of meditation and melancholy were those of a scholar rather than of a warrior. Serious, sombre and contemplative, it was as though life had intended him for academic matters rather than the sword, but whatever he did, she mused, Napoleon Bonaparte would do it to the full, so determined and thorough was he.

'Come back to bed, Napoleon,' she invited softly. Smiling, he threw off his air of absorption and returned to her outstretched arms.

In the morning he left her to the attention of her ladies-in-waiting, the Duchess de Montebello as Mistress of the Robes enjoying the task of adorning the Empress for the wedding. Despite the flurry of valets and equerries darting to and fro on urgent messages, the Duchess remained cool and critically efficient. The gown of purple velvet made by Leroy for the Empress and costing twelve thousand francs must be pinned and jewelled exactly so. And as if the heavily-encrusted gown cascading with diamonds were not enough, more diamonds were clasped about her throat before the cumbersome crown was placed on her head. Napoleon rushed in and out frequently to see all was well.

At last he too appeared fully dressed, taking Marie Louise's breath away.

'Napoleon! You look magnificent!' she cried. Accustomed to seeing him only in sombre, undecorated uniform, she could barely believe the sight; it was as though he had tried to cram on to his apparel every jewel he possessed. On his turban cap ran eight rows of diamonds, a further cluster holding in place each ostrich plume; his white satin coat boasted gold embroidery and more diamonds on the epaulettes; his shoe-buckles, his garters and the handle of his sword glittered with yet more diamonds; even his breeches and mantle bore encrustations of them. Proudly he took her hand and led her out to face the gasping spectators.

Marie Louise could barely walk, such a weight pressed on her brow and so heavy was her train. Outside St. Cloud rain was still falling as she entered the magnificent glass and gilt coach drawn by eight Andalusian horses. A cannonade of gunfire filled the air. Faces, myriads of faces peered through the glass sides of the coach, and then suddenly the sun shone.

Excited cheers filled the air. 'We are entering Paris,' Napoleon said. The coach passed under an unfinished Arc de Triomphe, and Marie Louise was entranced by the riot of colour, the decorations, sunlight glinted on spurting fountains —surely now the sun shone it was a happy omen after all? At the Tuileries the coach stopped.

Napoleon led her up the steps into a chamber where four Queens waited to bear Marie Louise's train, Caroline among them. Slowly they passed in state along the Grande Galerie to the Louvre, thousands of spectators in tiered seats either side gloating over the magnificent spectacle of their Emperor and Empress. Marie Louise glanced at Napoleon, wondering if he was feeling the strain of cumbersome crown and apparel as she was, but though he was pale he was smiling broadly.

Surrounded by admiring guests, Marie Louise could only gaze in wonder at the white satin ceiling and the walls encrusted with embroidered bees, the Imperial emblem. The Galerie had been transformed into a superb chapel of gold and silver brocade especially for the wedding.

Cardinal Fesch came forward to greet them. Marie Louise

saw Napoleon's pale face darken with anger as he quickly surveyed the room.

'The Cardinals, where are they?' he snapped. Murmurs and shaking heads declared that no one knew. Marie Louise's gaze followed his. Blank rows of seats indicated that the thirteen rebellious prelates had indeed declined to condone the ceremony, and her heart sank.

Nevertheless Napoleon knelt stubbornly by her side and made his vows. Timidly Marie Louise added hers. Throughout the singing and the benediction and the Te Deum she saw his expression, gloomy and absorbed, but as the ceremony ended and cries of 'Vive l'Empereur!' and Vive l'Impératrice!' filled the air, she saw his tension relax.

On the balcony he displayed her to the cheering crowds with a proud tenderness that touched Marie Louise. Alone again in the dimly-lit Tuileries he drew her close.

'Now, Louise, now you are finally, fully and irrevocably mine,' he murmured low. 'We shall be together for always.'

'For always, Napoleon.'

'Today you have borne yourself well, Louise, carrying that heavy crown for six hours and more. Lay it aside now. Come with me for I have a gift for you yet,' he whispered.

'Another? You have showered me with so many wonderful gifts already Napoleon.'

'But this, I think, will please you well. Come.'

As he took her hand Marie Louise followed obediently, wondering if it would be yet another jewel or a horse. Along passageways, so dark they had to be lamplit even in the daytime he led her, until they reached a door.

'In there,' he said tersely.

Wonderingly Marie Louise pushed open the door. Within a dog yelped, then hurled itself feverishly at her legs, yapping and wagging its tail in frenzied delight. Speechless with surprise she recognized Bijou, and bent joyfully to pick him up.

'Oh, Napoleon!' she murmured between tears at last. 'How kind! How thoughtful!'

'Go in to the room," Napoleon commanded. Obediently Marie Louise entered, hugging Bijou tearfully, and as the mist of tears receded she realized with a shock of delight that she was in her own boudoir in Vienna once more. Every etching, every trinket, the birdcages, even the rugs and chairs and table were her very own. Overcome, she turned to her husband, still scarcely able to believe her fortune.

'Oh Napoleon! All my beloved treasures, here in Paris! I am so happy! Oh, how kind you are!'

'Your thanks are due to Berthier, my dear. He told me how sorrowful you were to leave them all behind, especially Bijou.'

'Yet it was you who thought to bring them here for me. It was you who realized how bereft I would feel, and tried to make me feel at home among my dear, familiar belongings. Oh Napoleon! I shall be forever grateful to have a husband so considerate and thoughtful.'

'Then perhaps I am not such an Ogre after all?' he teased gently. Marie Louise blushed with shame under his searching gaze, recalling the terror of a child with a toy soldier and a bodkin.

'I thought so once, husband, but now I know better,' she answered gravely.

CHAPTER 8

PARIS, 1810

MARRIED life, Marie Louise discovered, was idyllic. True, life was very different in Paris from in Vienna, with its round of gaiety and ceremony compared to the stiff formality of home, but once one grew accustomed to the low décolletage of the women's gowns and the air of frivolity and pleasure, it was not so hard.

The strangest part of all was realizing that the illusion of Napoleon as a Monster was once and for all shattered. This amiable man with the solemnly considerate manner was so far removed from the great threatening bogey man of one's nursery days that it seemed incredible one could ever have been so gullible. That he adored her she knew beyond doubt. Once the festivities were ended he tried to keep her to himself entirely, as though unwilling to share a fraction of her with others.

For three weeks they sheltered alone together at Compiègne, staying abed late in the mornings and even preparing their own breakfast so as not to admit intrusive servants.

'I shall make the coffee,' Marie Louise declared.

'Chocolate. I always drink chocolate for breakfast.'

'And to eat?'

'Nothing.'

Marie Louise's blue eyes opened wide. 'But I am famished. Surely you will eat too?' Hunger, as ever, gnawed at her stomach. Always she had had a hearty appetite, and even a honeymoon was no reason to fast.

'Nothing for me. I never eat in the mornings. Food has little appeal for me. But you have; pray, leave the chocolate and play the piano for me, Louise.'

She played, he read to her aloud, she painted his portrait, and when they were at last obliged to admit others to their chamber they rode out together on horseback. It was a life of sheer bliss, and Marie Louise revelled in the ecstasy of wedded life.

'What are you doing, dearest?' she enquired, leaning over his shoulder one evening as he sat at his desk. The pen in his hand flew along so energetically that the tip pierced the paper.

'I am writing to your father to tell him how contented I am with my new wife.'

'What are you saying about me?'

'That you are all I desired—simple, unaffected, thrifty, and bonny as a country wench. Industrious, honest—what more can I say about you, you paragon of perfection?'

Marie Louise flushed with happiness. Almost before she could think, the words tripped from her tongue. 'Do I make you as happy as Josephine, then?'

She could have bitten her tongue when she saw his face cloud. It was stupid of her to remind him of the woman he loved and was forced to abjure. How could she believe herself as enticing as the lovely Josephine?

'Josephine was a marvellous woman, Louise, but she had none of your virtues. She was extravagant and idle, affected and often untruthful, and yet I loved her well. Let us speak no more of her.'

'I am sorry, Napoleon.' The tone of meekness in Marie Louise's voice evoked her husband's tenderness.

'It is I who should apologize for speaking to you so abruptly, dearest Louise. I did not mean to reproach you. Only know that a plain man such as I, who left home at the age of eight and have spent all the years since then in barracks and camps, I have need of a woman with the virtues you possess. I account myself extremely fortunate to have found you.'

The unaccustomed tone of humility in his voice touched Marie Louise deeply. He was such a great man, the most redoubtable figure in Europe, the Eagle whom none could prevent from swooping and seizing whatever his predatory eye desired, and yet he knelt at her feet like some idolatrous worshipper. She brushed away swiftly the insidious thought that it was perhaps only her lineage to which he paid homage, and seated herself opposite him at the desk.

'I too shall write to Papa and tell him how fortunate I am,' she said.

She felt his presence at her shoulder as she wrote :

'The more intimately one knows him, the better one learns to appreciate and love him,' she wrote neatly. . . . 'You will only understand this when you come to know the Emperor personally. Then you will see how good and lovable he is in private life, and what a noble-hearted man he is. I am persuaded that you would love him too.'

Napoleon cleared his throat quietly. 'Thank you, Louise. I hope my actions throughout our married life will always make you think thus.'

She smiled confidently. 'I am certain I shall, Napoleon.'

Life, thought the new Empress of the French, would be utterly sublime if only she could spend all her time with her adoring new husband, but there were times when matters of state obliged him, reluctantly, to hand her over to her ladies while he betook himself to his cabinet. Marie Louise cared little for her ladies' company, gay and frivolous creatures, scented and powdered and rather over-given to familiarity in her opinion. It was difficult to be at ease with people so far removed from her own retiring nature, and Marie Louise felt stiff and unnatural in their presence. The one lady she liked least, Queen Caroline, evidently was quick to sense her dislike and soon gave up her sycophantic attempts at friendship, for which Marie Louise was grateful.

Some ladies there were whom Marie Louise genuinely liked and whose company she enjoyed—the old Countess de Brignolle and Madame de Luçay, Marie Louise's lady of the wardrobe, Madame Saint-Aignon and above all, the Duchess de Montebello, her Mistress of the Robes. She, like all the others, had been Napoleon's choice, and at first Marie Louise had been prepared to hold her at a distance as she did the others who were too pressing and familiar. But the Duchess de Montebello was none of these; on the contrary, despite her bourgeois background she was modest and solicitous and above all, respectful. Marie Louise's confidence in her grew daily. It was to the Duchess she turned for advice on what to wear, what to say at a function, and how to address guests. As the young widow of the famed Marshal Lannes, killed at Essling fighting the Austrians, The Duchess commanded high respect at the Tuileries Court, and Marie Louise grew to value her friendship highly. Just as she had loved and trusted Madame Colloredo in the old days, she reflected wistfully, and the young Duchess's growing closeness began to atone for the sudden loss of Countess Lazansky.

'One must not permit familiarity,' The Duchess would say, her Madonna-like face marred by pursed lips on overhearing a lady's insolent chatter. Marie Louise agreed whole-heartedly, and one of the first rules she promulgated on her return from the honeymoon tour of the Lowlands was to render herself less accessible.

'I shall be occupied every morning, unavailable to receive guests until after lunch,' she declared. The Duchess nodded in agreement. 'None of my ladies is to enter my apartments at any time unless I send for her.'

'Quite right,' the Duchess asserted, sure of her own freedom to come and go. 'It is high time there was a certain distance and reserve about royalty, in my opinion, more hauteur, more dignity and less of this laxity.'

But when Leroy, the Court dressmaker, paid his respects to her Imperial Majesty, declaring her new gowns to be ready for fitting, Marie Louise found his gay, inconsequential chat rather too disrespectful. She surveyed the gowns displayed on wooden models critically.

'Are they not a little—décolleté?' she murmured anxiously. The Duchess de Montebello's tongue clicked in agreement. 'Yes, monsieur, I think a little low-cut in the bodice for my liking. I should prefer you to make them higher.'

Leroy's eyebrows arched high. 'But Your Majesty, it is the fashion! And moreover,' his grey eyes twinkled flatteringly, 'it would be a crime to conceal so lovely a throat as yours.'

Marie Louise heard the Duchess's gasp, and swiftly she turned on him, pointing majestically to the door as she spoke. 'Have this insolent fellow put out, she commanded firmly, 'and see to it he never appears here again.'

Bewildered, the well-meaning dressmaker was hustled out. Napoleon seemed amused when Marie Louise recounted the scene to him.

'I am glad you treated him sternly, my dear, for now all the Court will know you to be a regal creature not to be treated lightly. And I will not have you used so. Henceforth no man is to enter your apartments for any reason, save closely watched by your trusted ladies, and on no account will you receive a man alone.'

'I was not alone, Napoleon. Montebello was there, and others. Are they to stay with me when I have my music-lesson, then?'

'Of course.'

'And when Duplan dresses my hair?'

'Yes.'

So Marie Louise found herself forced more and more into the company of her ladies. Napoleon spent increasing hours in his cabinet, and Marie Louise began to fret about his prolonged absences from her side.

'What keeps you so long immured with the Duc de Cadore?' she would ask plaintively.

'My dear, I told you I do not wish to harass you with matters of State you cannot comprehend.'

'I only want to know what keeps you from me.'

'Many things. Domestic matters, international problems. You know my brother Louis is having trouble in Holland, and Sir Arthur Wellesley has landed English troops in Portugal. These matters necessitate work, my love, but let us talk now of other things. Shall we go and ride together?'

'It is nearly time for dinner, Napoleon.'

'Then afterwards?'

'Very well.'

She knew how he loved to gallop along beside her, the wind blowing for a time all worries from his mind. He loved the horse, a white Arab steed named le Vizir, which had been a gift from the Sultan of Turkey some ten years before, and which bore on its snowy flank the brand of the Imperial Crown and the letter N. Napoleon had a predilection for monogramming thus all that he possessed—his despatch cases, his pistols and sabres, his opera glasses and even his wine glasses. It was an oddly bourgeois idea, she thought; one of the evidences of his lowly birth she tried so hard to forget.

Dinner was a trial. Marie Louise ate enthusiastically as always, trying not to notice that Napoleon ate only two of the meat courses. Soup, three entrées, four hors d'oeuvres, two sweet dishes and four desserts he ignored completely, and while Marie Louise ate on happily he rose and stood by the fireplace watching her and sipping a glass of Chambertin. At last she finished, pushing away her plate with a satisfied sigh. Napoleon put down his glass.

'Shall we ride out now. my love?'

She shook her head. 'Later, perhaps. I do not feel like riding now.'

'You eat too much. No wonder you suffer such frequent attacks of indigestion.'

Marie Louise made no answer; he sounded so like the reproachful voice of the Austrian Empress, her mother, calling her a Naschkatzerl, a glutton. She would not mention the half-dozen cream tarts she had ordered to be sent up to her room shortly. He was watching her closely.

'At what hour will you ride then?'

'Oh, not today, I think. Tomorrow perhaps.'

'Then I must return to my despatches.'

She watched him go, and this time she did not feel neglected. She felt too queasy to care. Perhaps she had over-eaten after all.

The Duchess de Montebello was all concern. 'Oh, Your Majesty, do let me give you a dose of my medicine. It is marvellous for indigestion.'

Marie Louise drank it obediently. Within an hour cramp seized her stomach, causing her to cry out in pain. The

Duchess was panic-stricken, but Napoleon had to be informed.

He strode angrily into Marie Louise's chamber, his face furious and the Duc de Cadore fluttering behind him.

'Fetch Dr Corvisart at once,' he thundered, and bent low over Marie Louise, smoothing the fair hair back from her sweatsoaked brow.

'What caused this, Louise?'

'The medicine Montebello gave me, I think.'

Napoleon glared round at the unfortunate Duchess. 'Madame,' he said icily, 'do you not know the Court etiquette? If Her Majesty requires treatment it is her doctor's privilege to present it to her, not yours. Never presume to meddle with Her Majesty's health again.'

Marie Louise saw the Duchess, white-faced and wringing her hands, nod convulsively. Dr Corvisant appeared and bent over the Empress, but over his shoulder Marie Louise could see Napoleon's anguished face and suddenly the realization came to her that he had misunderstood. Her nausea he had taken as a sign of what he longed for. He believed her pregnant!

Muttered words between Napoleon and the doctor on the far side of the chamber indicated to Marie Louise that Napoleon was being disabused of this idea, and she felt guilty. Obviously his hopes had been raised after three months of marriage, and after all, this had been openly acknowledged as the reason for his new marriage.

Miserably, Marie Louise grappled with her colic and was glad when they all went out leaving her alone at last. That night Napoleon reappeared, dressing-gowned and freshly-shaven and smelling strongly of eau-de-cologne and jasmine. With a start of recollection Marie Louise remembered the same scent lurking in Schönbrunn long ago.

'I am sorry, Louise. I was a little abrupt with you today,' he muttered sharply.

'No matter. I am well again now.'

'I want you to know I love you despite my manner. I cannot help my brusque ways.'

'I know. Come to bed, Napoleon.'

He sat on the edge of the bed, taking her hand. 'Foolishly perhaps, I believed you *enceinte,* and would have killed Montebello for her presumption if she had caused you harm. You know how much I long to present an Eaglet to the nation.'

'Yes, my dear. And so we shall, soon.' Throwing back the coverlets, Marie Louise beckoned him into bed. Napoleon, tossing aside his dressing gown, leapt in.

It was surprising how often the Empress's attacks of indigestion began to occur from then on, almost daily, it seemed. Napoleon, unwilling to be misled again, continued with his urgent affairs while Marie Louise fretted.

'I shall arrange a little ball for you this evening and accompany you,' he would say in an attempt to stay her reproaches.

'But what shall I do all day?'

'Oh—go visit the art gallery with Montebello, or go to a concert. There is much to see in Paris.'

'I do not like going out without you, Napoleon. I feel so— gauche and insecure without you.'

'Nonsense, my dear.' His burst of laughter ridiculed the notion that a Hapsburg princess could ever lack self-confidence. And so she continued to have to amuse herself, by day at least, and would probably have resigned herself to the idea if a sudden, horrifying rumour had not burst upon the peace of the Tuileries. It was Montebello who caught the whisper and bore it to Marie Louise.

'Josephine has returned from exile and is living at Malmaison. She keeps court there, surrounding herself with many of your courtiers, Your Majesty. Hortense, her daughter, is there constantly.'

'So she should,' replied Marie Louise coolly. 'Her place is by her mother since her father is dead. And why should not Josephine return? She means us no harm, I am sure.'

'They say she wrote to Napoleon to settle her outstanding bills for her, and he has done so.'

'He is a kind man.' Marie Louise could not bring herself to voice even to Montebello, the shock of hearing he had corresponded with Josephine secretly.

'And what is more, Your Majesty, he is in the habit of visiting her at Malmaison.'

'What? Now?' There was no disguising the shock now.

'Yes, but let me hasten to add he meets her in the grounds and walks and talks with her there, within view of the courtiers. He never enters the palace.'

Montebello's words plagued Marie Louise for the remainder of the day. Napoleon loved her she was certain of it, so what reason was there for such secrecy? All the world knew he had adored Josephine, but he had put her aside for Marie Louise of his own free will. There was nothing in these clandestine meetings, Marie Louise argued, but if not, why were they clandestine? There was only one way to resolve this matter —to ask Napoleon himself.

But Napoleon seemed preoccupied and broody, and Marie Louise kept silent. In any case, she felt queasy again and if she roused him from his absorption he would be sure to notice and quiz her. So the question about Josephine went unasked, and whenever Napoleon rode out from the Tuileries Marie Louise watched from a window and wept. She wept not only from misery that so short an idyllic union was already ended, but that she had failed her father also, for if Emperor Francis came to hear of Josephine he would be heartbroken.

Miserably Marie Louise rang the bell and ordered the Duchess de Montebello to have a consoling box of Italian chocolates sent up to her chamber at once.

CHAPTER 9

PARIS, 1810–1811

NAPOLEON BONAPARTE felt himself a rather fortunate fellow in his choice of a new wife, for Marie Louise was all he had hoped for—dutiful and obedient, yet passionately responsive in a way her cool exterior had not led one to expect. Yes, he thought speculatively as his appreciative glance rested on her ample curves and slender waist, it had been a shrewd move to ally himself to her noble descent although it had meant abnegating Josephine's voluptuous charms.

Josephine. His dark eyes softened at the thought of his one-time wife, for she had been a creature of violent emotion and passion, an earthy woman who understood his needs and satisfied them well. It had been heart-breaking to behold her hysterical sobbing and pleading when the wrench of parting came, but he would always honour and care for her, paying her debts however extravagant she might continue, for the sake of what once had been between them. If only she had been fertile. . . .

But still, matters had turned out for the best after all, for his sons would be nobly-born, and Marie Louise was no bad substitute for Josephine's passion. The court might consider her cold and aloof, but he knew the coolness veiled only her unsureness, the aloofness her passion.

And how nobly she bore herself, this Austrian princess! Unlike Josephine, whom anyone, however lowly, could approach and befriend, Marie Louise held everyone at arm's length, even his sisters Pauline and Caroline. Pauline cared little, preoccupied as she was with her many lovers, but he felt Caroline had been somewhat piqued at her failure before returning at last to Naples with her husband.

But it was on the night of the great ball thrown by Prince Schwarzenberg at the Austrian Embassy that Napoleon beheld his bride at her noblest, and the memory was to remain long in his mind.

The Austrian Ambassador, anxious to equal the Emperor's sister Pauline's recent ball in splendour, had enlarged his Embassy by building an enormous wooden ballroom in the gardens, connected to the house by a fine gallery. Both ballroom and gallery were draped in striped canvas to conceal the wood, then hung with satin and gauze draperies and lighted by a thousand chandeliers. Flowers spilled everywhere, millions of blooms, their scent pulsating in the still, hot July air. Napoleon, escorting his gorgeously-apparelled Empress, was exultant, his customary sober manner melting for once into infectious gaiety. At his side Marie Louise smiled shyly.

'Come, sit by me on the dais,' Napoleon murmured as he led her to sit on the thrones surrounded by half the crowned heads of Europe. There she could be seen by all, flushed and radiant and looking her prettiest. Laughter tinkled above the music of the orchestra, guests were smiling as they took hands to dance the quadrille, everything reflected happiness and enjoyment.

Metternich drew Napoleon aside to converse. From across the room Napoleon's dark eyes watched Marie Louise's pretty face in pleasure. Suddenly he saw her stiffen and the colour fled from her cheeks. He followed her wide-eyed gaze to the window, and saw the billowing gauze curtain caught in the soft breeze, its tip hovering over a candelabra and the tongue of the flame which licked slowly about it. Before he could cry out the tongue had multiplied itself a thousandfold.

'Fire!' a voice cried. 'Fire! Fire!' Panic and consternation spread instantly throughout the room, replacing in a second the merriment and gaiety of a moment before. Measured dance steps changed instantly into a rush of terror towards the doors, screams replaced the laughter and music, and stark fear filled the eyes of every guest. Napoleon rose to his feet and saw Marie Louise still sat, composed but white-faced, on her flimsy throne. Instantly he lost sight of her as his Imperial Guard, disciplined to a man, closed in about him.

'Let me pass!' he commanded.

'Keep close, Sire, lest it is an Austrian plot,' one of the Guard replied, his sabre drawn and ready.

'The Empress, you fool! Let me get to her!' Napoleon roared, pushing the man aside in his haste. Flames roared about his ears, devouring savagely the fragile gauze, and as Napoleon fought his way through the seething, fighting, terrified mob he could see Marie Louise still seated, alone, on the dais.

Hysteria raged as fiercely as the flames, men trampling on women's fallen bodies as they fought in terror to reach the exits. Metternich pressed close to Napoleon's side, ducking to avoid a falling, blazing beam.

'Sire, I know the construction of this hall,' Metternich cried above the crackle and screaming. 'It is doomed, but there are many exits. Follow me and you will be safe.'

'I must reach the Empress first!'

Reaching the dais Napoleon leapt forward. Marie Louise took his outstretched hand calmly, a faint flicker of a smile on her white face. What calm courage the girl possessed, Napoleon thought as he led her through the mob. He had seen seasoned soldiers face a crisis far less nobly.

They reached the garden safely, but within the blazing building the cries of terror-crazed guests could be heard still above the roar of the inferno.

'A carriage!' Napoleon thundered. 'Let the Empress be taken at once to St. Cloud, while I see what can be done here.'

Marie Louise showed the first sign of agitation then. 'Oh, Napoleon! Please come with me! Do not go back in there!' she cried.

The coach appeared. Napoleon bundled her in unceremoniously and clambered in after her. At the Place Louis Quatorze he ordered the coach to stop.

'I will go back,' he said tersly. Marie Louise looked terrified.

'Oh no, Napoleon! Please! I could not bear to think of you risking your life! Come with me I beg!'

'Go home, Louise, I shall follow soon.' So saying, he was gone.

He did what he could but the fire took a terrible toll. By morning only a smouldering heap of ashes remained of the once-magnificent ballroom, and a mound of charred corpses that had once been his friends. Prince Schwarzenberg was grief-stricken, and Napoleon mourned with him for the loss of his lovely Princess Schwarzenberg who would soon have borne him their ninth child.

Napoleon's steps were leaden as he returned to St. Cloud. He had not missed the muttered whispers among the rescuers at that ghastly scene, the superstitious recollection of another fire bringing death and disaster forty years ago, at another fête arranged for an Austrian Archduchess whose end was terrible. He had realized their implication, those malicious tongues—that this was for Marie Louise as evil an omen as that other fire had been for Marie Antoinette.

D

'Stupid, credulous fools!' he muttered to himself as he strode rapidly to Marie Louise's chamber. At his knock she leapt to her feet and rushed to throw herself into his arms.

'Oh Napoleon! You are safe! Oh, thank God!' she cried, her lip trembling in an effort not to weep. He smiled down at her tenderly, remembering once again how bravely she had conducted herself amid the terror-crazed mêlée. Taking her hands, he led her to sit beside him in a window seat.

'Was it—terrible?' she whispered at last.

He nodded. 'Princess Schwarzenberg was one of the victims. She was *enceinte,* you know.'

Marie Louise hung her head, her gaze avoiding his. 'Oh how awful! How can I ever tell the Prince now of my own joy?'

Napoleon eyed her curiously. 'What do you mean, Louise? What joy?

The blue eyes looked up now, directly into his. 'I would have chosen a better moment, Napoleon, but I never could keep a secret. Dr. Corvisant has just examined me.'

Napoleon's dark eyes grew alarmed. 'You are not harmed, Louise? Tell me you are not?'

'No, dearest, but the good doctor examined me to be certain. I told him then of certain—symptoms—and he assured me we can now rejoice. You see, I too am *enceinte.*'

Napoleon's eyes widened, and as understanding dawned, a look of pure joy irradiated his dark countenance. He gripped her shoulders ecstatically. 'Louise, are you sure? Are you positive? There can be no mistake?'

She shook her head smilingly. 'No, my dear, there is no mistake.'

He kissed her long and soundly, then, unable to contain his delirious joy, he leapt to his feet and paced about the chamber, talking in great energetic bursts, picking up the poker to stab viciously at the coals, and coming back to her side at last.

'Oh Louise! Oh, my Empress! I am so proud of you! I shall love and treasure you always, you who are to bear my son! I shall cradle you like a fragile blossom and grant you all your little heart ever desired! Oh my precious!'

Finding speech inadequate, he grew silent at last, but his restless fingers traced the outline of her face and neck, and come to rest at last wonderingly on her stomach.

'There lies my son, the future King of Rome,' he murmured. 'Nurture him well, Louise, for in him lie all my hopes.'

'Rest assured I will, Napoleon,' she replied contentedly. It was only as they lay side by side in the great bed, Napoleon's arm encircling Marie Louise, that he remembered the fire and its tragic consequences. It was surprising how swiftly good fortune could drive ill from the memory, but though Napoleon mourned still for the loss of his subjects, his mind was already busy, planning and scheming for the advent of his child. Marie Louise must be made supremely happy during the critical time ahead; Josephine must go. She must leave Malmaison and he would visit her no more. Moreover her initials which still ornamented the chambers of the Tuileries must be erased. Whatever might upset Marie Louise's now very important personage must be attended to forthwith. Nothing must be allowed to disturb her peace of mind, for above all else Napoleon longed for a perfect, robust son to lead the world after him.

'I want to display you to the whole world, my dearest wife,' he told her proudly. 'I want everyone to know that you are soon to bear my child.'

Marie Louise raised blank blue eyes. 'But there is nothing yet for them to see,' she demurred. 'Oh Napoleon, I would so love some peaches! Would you order some to be sent up at once?'

'So soon after dinner? You will be sick again, my love. I think the opera tomorrow night, then the Opera-Comique the following night. Then perhaps a diplomatic reception here at the Tuileries, and let me see, what else? The Théatre Française, I think, and perhaps a visit or two to the library and museums. By then everyone should know.'

He was totally immersed in the thought of the child, of letting the world know of his joy. Marie Louise shrugged and went on satisfying her sudden, capricious cravings that they said every pregnant woman experienced, enjoying the solicitude Napoleon lavished on her. Though it seemed a trifle undignified to stand up in the imperial box at the theatre, ostensibly to acknowledge the cheers but really to let the people see her figure as Napoleon demanded, she did as she was bidden. After all, her husband was as devoted to her now as any besotted lover could be, even forsaking his cabinet business to attend her. And one day he even drove her to Malmaison. No Josephine now resided there. Marie Louise's eyes clouded with grateful tears. For her sake he had even discontinued his friendship with his former wife—what greater proof of his love could he show?

To Victoire, now herself married and revelling in the name of Madame de Crenneville, Marie Louise wrote happily.

'My own marriage is unexpectedly happy. I wish you, my dear friend, a fate akin to my own, in having a loving husband and the prospect of a child. What more could any woman want of life?'

The days passed lazily and contentedly. Marie Louise continued to indulge her passions for reading, collecting coins and medals, in preparing the vast layette for her coming child, and in eating and sleeping and eating again. Gradually her body thickened and swelled, and Napoleon's ecstatic gaze watched the progress joyfully.

'No more dancing or riding,' he pronounced firmly. Marie Louise's eyes widened in dismay.

'But I love riding, Napoleon!' she protested.

'I know my love, but we can take no chances. After the child is born you may ride again as much as you choose.'

She knew what he feared—that her own mother had lost her life in childbirth and he had no intention that harm should come to her. Acknowledging his concern with a tender smile, she argued no more. He was so good to her, so kind and gentle. Only very occasionally did he desert her now to debate with his ministers in his cabinet, and only then because the war with England was creating economic problems, and Louis in Holland was proving troublesome again. Napoleon had even threatened to send an army to subdue his rebellious brother. But still, at the end of an hour or two of debate Napoleon would return to her side and she watched with pleasure how his sombre, preoccupied look would melt away as his eyes rested on her figure.

'Come, my love, and see what the citizens of Paris have presented us for our child,' he murmured happily one day when he rejoined her. Marie Louise followed him dutifully, wishing he would not walk so fast while she lumbered along behind. He paused and took her hand, throwing open a door with his free hand. 'Behold.'

Accustomed as she was to Napoleon's extravagance in every way, Marie Louise could not help clapping her hand to her mouth in surprise. There, in the centre of the room, stood a huge silver-gilt cradle, ornamented with mother-of-pearl and Napoleon's emblem of golden bees.

'Oh, how beautiful!' she cried, coming closer to see it the better. 'Look, a figure holding a wreath of laurels, and here, above it, your star! And oh, what beautiful draperies and magnificent lace!'

'Prudhon designed it,' Napoleon replied proudly. 'There is Justice, see? and Fame, and Strength. And here, an Eaglet.'

Marie Louise smiled, inwardly hoping that she would indeed provide Napoleon with the Eaglet he craved. Time was passing swiftly. It could not be long now, for already the trees outside the palace windows were in bud. By late March the Eaglet was due to appear.

'It is time we made ready,' Napoleon announced. 'Madame de Montebello and Dr. Dubois must move into the Tuileries at once so as to be in readiness.'

Somehow the words had a terrible finality about them to Marie Louise's sensitive ears. Suddenly it was borne in on her that the birth now was inevitable—and imminent. Secret dread invaded her whole being and she felt panic-stricken. Napoleon, feeling her shudder, sent her lady to fetch a wrap, snapping at the unfortunate woman for letting Her Majesty risk a chill at such a critical time.

One March evening she sat at her dressing table and allowed Montebello to dress her hair before going down to the evening's play in the Tuileries. She felt strangely remote and an odd twinge kept nagging the middle of her back. Montebello was quick to notice her cool, offhanded manner. 'Do you not feel well, Your Majesty?'

Diffidently Marie Louise explained the odd sensation. Madame's face stiffened. 'I think I had best call Dr. Dubois, if you will permit,' she said quickly. Dubois came running. The examination over, he straightened.

'It would be best if your guests were sent home this evening, Your Majesty,' he announced solemnly.

'But why? I am not ill.'

'No, indeed not. But you are in labour. Let His Imperial Majesty be informed at once.'

Montebello fled. Marie Louise lay white-faced but composed. So now it was to happen. Now nothing could prevent it. Then a wonderful thought caused her tight lips to relax and curve into a tender smile. When the next pain came, Marie Louise fought down the momentary panic and tried to reassure herself with an uplifting thought. By the morning, God willing, she would be able to present Napoleon with that which he desired above all else. A child.

CHAPTER 10

PARIS, 1811

THROUGHOUT the night Marie Louise's cries echoed through the Luxemburg Palace. By morning Napoleon's exultation was diminishing, for his young wife was not enduring the protracted process of childbirth as easily as he had anticipated.

'The birth is a difficult one, I fear,' the agitated Dr. Dubois admitted at last, pausing in his labours to exchange a few words with Napoleon outside the birth-chamber.

'What can we do?' Napoleon demanded, his normal self-confidence flickering. For half the night he had sat patiently wiping the sweat from Marie Louise's brow and soothing her anguished cries with encouraging words.

Dubois shrugged feebly. 'It is no fault of the Empress's. She does as I ask her but it seems the child is reluctant to come. If this persists much longer I fear she will become too exhausted, and the child also.'

'Is she in danger?' the Emperor's voice was low.

Dubois hung his head. From the chamber another agonized scream rent the air. Napoleon paled.

'The baby lies badly, and it will require a surgical operation to deliver it,' Dubois said quietly. 'The Empress cannot hope to give birth naturally.'

'You do not answer me. Is she in danger?' Napoleon repeated fiercely.

'It is possible either mother or child will not survive the

operation. If Her Imperial Majesty should survive, it is highly unlikely she will ever bear another child. I can tell you it is a boy-child.'

Napoleon was silent for a moment, his mind racing. His son, the King of Rome, was so near, and yet he might not live. And if Louise lived, there would be no more sons. Did ever man have more terrible a choice to make? Dubois' anxious eyes seemed to indicate he knew what the choice should be, for young Archduchesses were easier to come by than heirs to the French Imperial throne. Napoleon faced him squarely.

'The child is of secondary consideration, do you understand that, Dubois? You are to treat the Empress just as though she were any woman of the Rue Saint-Martin. There you would have no hesitation in saving the mother first. Do so now. You can do no more.'

Dubois sped back to the bedside, and shortly after Napoleon followed. Marie Louise writhed and moaned in pain on the bed, and even Napoleon's gentle caresses had no effect on her. At the sight of Dubois' scalpels and forceps she screamed out in terror.

'Ach! Mein Gott! What are you going to do?'

'Be easy, Louise,' Napoleon murmured, his voice choking in sympathy with the girl's terror and pain. 'Dubois will soon ease your agony.'

'Must I be sacrificed because I am Empress? Oh Napoleon! Do not kill me!' Marie Louise's voice trailed away in a diminuendo of pain, her eyes huge with fear. Napoleon could bear no more. As Dubois picked up a knife and Marie Louise's screams tore round the room, he hastened out.

Outside he sat silent, sweat beading his brow and his hands clasped tight to prevent the terrible shuddering that gripped his body. Oh God, it was so cruel; Louise, barely a woman at nineteen, yet she stood so near the gates of Death, her agony indescribable. Poor Louise. Willingly now he would forego his child to save her from further suffering.

At last Dubois' pale face appeared at the door, and he nodded to Napoleon to come.

'It is over,' he said softly. 'The Empress lives.'

Dazed and trembling, Napoleon rose and followed him into the room. Marie Louise lay, white-faced and tearstained, and Napoleon hastened to enfold her in his arms.

'Dearest Louise!'

He was barely aware of the doctors and nurses under Dubois' charge and Madame de Montesquiou, who would have been the child's governess. Figures moved and merged about him, but he was conscious only of Louise's trembling, exhausted body in his arms.

'It is over, Louise, and it is morning already. Sleep now, my love,' he said softly, disengaging himself from her arms. Behind him there was a flutter of movement. He glanced around. A woman held a little bundle in her arms, and with a stab of pain he realized it was the corpse of his child. Why had they not removed it by now, he thought angrily. Had not poor Louise suffered enough torment without seeing this reminder of her fruitless travail?

Madame de Montesquiou wrenched the bundle from the nurse's hands and, uncovering the little body, slapped it harshly. Then, taking a spoonful of brandy from a glass, she forced it between the tiny blue lips.

'You are wasting your time, Madame,' Napoleon snapped. Unheeding, she called for hot towels and wrapped the little red body tightly. Napoleon turned away with a bitter sigh, glad at least that Marie Louise's eyes were closed.

A faint cry disturbed the silent tension in the air. Napoleon glanced up, disbelieving, yet a faint quiver of hope flickering in his breast. Was it possible? Marie Louise's head rolled over and the blue eyes stared wide. Another cry, and then another rang out, and every soul in the room stood motionless. Dr. Dubois was the first to break the tableau, hastening to Madame de Montesquiou's side.

'He lives,' he murmured incredulously, and then triumphantly he cried. 'He lives!' For a moment Napoleon stood immobile, unable to believe the words, then he leapt to peer into the bundle Madame was holding with a tender smile. A minute red face, puckered indignantly, was emitting fierce squeals of protest.

'Alive! My son is alive!' Napoleon's voice croaked in emotion. Marie Louise's staring eyes creased into a feeble smile. Leaving his long-desired son to kneel at the bedside, Napoleon took her hand.

'Our son lives, ma bonne Louise. We have our King of Rome after all. God bless you, sweetheart.'

He kissed her fingertips and felt her grasp tighten. For her sake too he was glad, for now her suffering was not in vain after all.

'Bring the King of Rome to the Empress,' he commanded at last. Proudly and reverently Madame de Montesquiou advanced and laid the precious bundle alongside his mother. Radiant joy shone on the faces of both parents and, bowing low, the retinue of doctors and nurses and attendants left the chamber to allow the royal couple to savour their moment of bliss.

Twenty-one guns announced to Paris the arrival of the King of Rome on March 20th, 1811, and at once the city went mad with joy. That same evening Napoleon proudly carried his son to the Chapel of the Tuileries for his preliminary christening, and the important little scrap of humanity was named Napoleon Francis Charles Joseph Bonaparte.

The following day Marie Louise, beginning to recover from her ordeal, enquired of Napoleon how their son fared.

'He is magnificent, Louise. Today he held his first court, lying in his beautiful cradle he received dignitaries and diplomats, and I invested our little King with the Legion of Honour.'

'Did he cry?'

'Cry? Not he! I think Madame Auchard had fed him well first, for he lay there as fat and contented as a kitten.'

'He is not fat! He is beautiful,' Marie Louise commented happily, for in truth he was. Plump, and with fine golden hair and delicate colouring, she fancied he bore quite a striking resemblance to herself, but before she could voice the thought, Madame de Montesquiou entered with the child. 'Give him to me,' commanded Napoleon, and Marie Louise saw his proud, intent gaze as he peered at the baby. 'You know, Louise, he is very like me,' he commented at last. 'He has my mouth and eyes, don't you agree?' He handed the squirming infant to her. Marie Louise took him apprehensively, fearful lest she should drop him.

'He is heavy,' she ventured.

'He weighs nine pounds.' Napoleon's voice rang with pride. 'But give him to Montesquiou—she knows best how to handle him.'

Marie Louise surrendered him to Madame's capable hands. As she was to discover in the months to come, Madame de Montesquiou and the buxom young wetnurse, Madame Auchard, would between them take all the care of the child upon themselves, and she would have but little to do with him.

But for the moment she was content. It was pleasant to have a flat stomach once more and to revel in congratulations and Napoleon's adoring gratitude, pleasanter by far now that the agony of the birth she had dreaded so much was behind her.

Montebello fussed anxiously about her, plumping her pillows and making sure her mistress was comfortable.

'I am indeed a lucky woman,' Marie Louise confided dreamily. 'To think I once feared Napoleon so much, yet now I am perfectly content with him. He pampers me so, surrounding me with love and luxury.'

'Which is no more than your due, Your Majesty,' Montebello purred. 'You have given His Majesty his Eaglet—and such an Eaglet! Paris is wild with joy.'

But no-one's joy could outshine Napoleon's; glowing with pride he would snatch moments from his cabinet to rush to the nursery and seize his son from his nurse, pacing about as he gazed at the tiny face in ecstasy.

'Nothing is too good for my King of Rome,' he would breathe fervently. 'Nothing but the best for my son.'

So it was that, once Marie Louise was recovered and the Court was to move from the Tuileries to St. Cloud, that the little King travelled not with his parents, but in his own magnificent equipage, surrounded by his own suite.

Marie Louise wrote to her father of her adorable son.

'He is very strong for five weeks. . . . He spends all day in the garden. The Emperor takes a lot of notice of his son. He carries him about in his arms.'

Which was more than she was allowed to do, she reflected a little sadly. They accounted her, at nineteen, too inexperienced to take charge of him, preferring the proven capabilities of Madame de Montesquiou. It was a bitter thought that after so much travail to bring him into the world, he would grow up closer to his governess than to his own mother.

The wistful thoughts vanished when Ferdi suddenly arrived from Vienna.

'As heir to the Hapsburg crown, I come to bring greetings to the young heir to the French crown,' he laughed, taking Marie Louise in his arms in a warm embrace. Marie Louise was delighted to see her brother, now grown to a handsome young man of eighteen, though he still looked as nervous and pallid as ever.

'Are you happy, Luischen?' he asked her. 'We thought in Vienna perhaps you were only pretending in order to make us happy.' He eyed her keenly, taking in her features, still pale from her recent ordeal and her figure, decidedly thinner.

'I am happy, Ferdi. You know there is no dissimulation in me.'

'I am relieved, I confess it. Now I can report it to Papa— and also that your son is remarkably like you.'

No sooner had Ferdi left Paris to bear the good tidings to Vienna than Napoleon sprang another surprise on Marie Louise.

'A triumphal tour of the Netherlands in the autumn when you have recovered your strength,' he declared, seated by the fire in his favourite claw-footed armchair.

'And your affairs of state?' Marie Louise questioned.

'Can await my return. We shall not take the boy, of course, for he is too young. Montesquiou and his wet nurse will take complete charge of him during our absence.'

'Very well,' Marie Louise's small voice replied. Her duty was to obey, never to question, but as she watched Napoleon sitting gazing into the fire in his olive-green Chasseur of the Guard uniform, his ink-spattered white kerseymere breeches and the purple Legion of Honour ribbon spread across his white waistcoat, she knew he thought only of the Bonaparte destiny. Love her he might, but he would never understand a mother's feelings. Such a little scrap, but already her son was being weaned from her and given to others to tend. Marie Louise could only comfort herself in the knowledge that, as Francis had solemnly bidden, she was obeying her husband implicitly.

'A grand State christening in June, I think,' Napoleon was murmuring to the fireplace. 'Cardinal Fesch will officiate and for the godparents I shall choose King Joseph of Spain and your father, and Caroline and Madame Mère.'

Marie Louise made no reply, for none was expected of her. Napoleon would arrange every detail of life for their son. After a moment's silence Napoleon spoke again.

'But before exposing him before so many people I think it would be best to have him vaccinated. Yes, I must discuss with Corvisant and Dubois—I think Dr Husson shall perform the operation.'

Marie Louise's alarm caused her to cry out before she could think. 'Vaccination? Oh, but Napoleon it is such a dangerous operation! It is a very new and unproven idea, I understand. Must he undergo such a risk?'

'I have decided.' Napoleon's voice was coolly determined, and Marie Louise knew better than to argue. Instead she kept her anxiety to herself, gnawing until the critical day came. In agitation she waited in her own boudoir until news came.

'It is over,' Montebello reported as soon as it was done. 'Dr. Husson punctured his arm three times and administered the vaccine taken from Madame Auchard's little girl's arm.'

'Did he cry, Montebello?'

'No. He was suckling Auchard's breast all the time and is very content.'

Twelve days later His Majesty the King of Rome was feverish, but none would allow Marie Louise near him. They purged him with chicory and peach-flower, and as the scabs fell off, he began to recover. Marie Louise, kept from his side, felt more estranged from her child than ever.

Was it her imagination, she wondered, or was Napoleon less attentive than hitherto? Certainly she saw less of him, preoccupied as he always was either with affairs of state or with the baby. Sadly she commented to Madame de Montbello on her loneliness.

'Madame de Montesquiou considers the baby her own,' Montebello replied with a thin-lipped smile. 'She allows no-one else but Auchard and His Majesty near. It is as His Majesty wishes it.'

'But I see little of Napoleon either,' Marie Louise replied. 'Oh, Montebello, do you know how I would really like to live? I would have none of this stuffy Court ceremonial, only Napoleon all to myself, and the baby, and be free to walk in the Vienna woods without eyes continually staring at us, and listen to Viennese music and eat Viennese pastries and delicious coffee. Oh, to be able to be oneself, simple and free and not chained by duty!'

'One must be content with one's destiny, Madame.'

'I know it. And I should be glad Napoleon now seems to care more for being alone with his wife and son than for grand ceremonial as he used. I have much to be grateful for, have I not, Montebello?'

It was no exaggeration. Napoleon did hasten often from his cabinet to the nursery to snatch the baby up, toss him delightedly in the air to Marie Louise's secret alarm, and roll over and over with him on the floor. Marie Louise saw how Napoleon's dark eyes gleamed in pleasure as the baby would reach for his sabre, and he would comment 'Ah, my little King of Rome will be a fighter too. He too will hold what he desires.'

As the baby began to grow older, to crawl and then to toddle, Napoleon's delight in him seemed to increase daily. Even less now could he bear to be parted from the boy, dandling him on his knee as he worked at his papers or building up the blocks of wood he used to represent his regiments on the battlefield for the baby to knock down, crowing with delight. Marie Louise began to feel even more isolated.

'I know the intense family feeling of all the Bonapartes, Montebello, and so it is natural my husband feels so close to the boy,' she would confide sadly.

'Indeed, Your Majesty. It is a trait of the Corsicans. Madame Mère watches all her brood with a hawklike eye; and your husband is her favourite.'

'But I feel lonely, Montebello. After my levée I ride or paint or play music while my husband is occupied, and Montesquiou guards my baby jealously. I would there was something I could do, something creative and useful—but what?'

Concern glowed in Madame de Montebello's eyes. 'I know just how you feel, Madame, and I too would feel unhappy in your shoes. Montesquiou is trying to steal your baby's love. The Bonapartes shut you out from their clan as an alien who is better-born and not of their blood. Madame Mère is determined to guide her children the way she sees fit, and it is she who truly rules France. As for Pauline—she is no better than she ought to be, that lustful one. Society, led by such as she, is a cesspool of filth and iniquity. You are better off without her friendship.'

The two women, seated on a couch by the open window, glanced up as a shadow fell upon them. Napoleon entered through the French window, his sombre eyes flashing. Montebello leapt up anxiously, fearful lest he had overheard. Marie Louise too rose, guilt fluttering in her heart.

'My dear! Is the Council ended so soon?' she exclaimed in surprise. On Tuesdays he was usually kept late in debate. Napoleon turned to the Duchess de Montebello.

'My dear Madame,' he said smoothly, but the fire in his eyes belied his calm words, 'pray continue your charming account of my family. It seems it is you I have to thank for poisoning Her Majesty's mind against them. In future I shall request that you desist from such interesting tales, otherwise I shall have to see to it that my orders are obeyed.'

Marie Louise saw the Duchess's shoulders tremble, but whether with fear or rage she did not know. Montebello withdrew swiftly. Napoleon turned and took Marie Louise in his arms.

'I hope you paid her no attention, ma bonne. Remember, she is jealous and she hates me, so she thinks to influence you against me.'

'Oh no, Napoleon! She cannot believe that! She knows well how I love and respect you. Only. . . .'

'Only what, Louise?'

'Only sometimes I am so lonely, so—useless. I would there was something I could do to help you. You are so clever, so brilliant. All the world holds you in respect, but I am a clumsy, useless thing.'

It was abysmally futile and far from the truth. But how else could Marie Louise express her frustration and deprivation at the long absences from both her husband and child? Napoleon eyed her thoughtfully.

'It may be that I am shrewd, but remember Louise that aptitude is God-given; application is self-imposed. Together they make brilliance, but we mortals can claim neither the credit nor the blame. The choice is God's.'

Marie Louise sighed. 'If only I too had a strong point like you Napoleon.'

He smiled warmly and squeezed her close. 'You have, my dear. Your forte is your obedience, Louise, your sense of duty. Few have this quality, to the measure that you have, and that is highly to be admired. Come now, my love, it is time for our drive.'

Amid the amber leaves of autumn the Emperor of France and his Empress left on their triumphal tour of the Netherlands. Marie Louise hugged her baby tenderly before relinquishing him to Montesquiou's eager arms, but in the eventful, glittering weeks that followed the yearning for him began to pain her less. But on the misty November day when the great glass and gilt coach rumbled back into Paris, Marie Louise's heart was buoyant at the thought of seeing him, his chubby little arms outstretched in greeting, and she could barely wait for the moment his aja brought him to them.

In the vestibule Madame de Montesquiou was waiting with the boy. Napoleon flung aside his cloak and hastened forward, his eyes glowing with pure pleasure at the sight of the sleepy-eyed toddler in her arms.

'How has he fared, Montesquiou?'

'Well, Your Majesty. But listen a moment—say Papa, chéri, say Papa to your father,' she coaxed the boy.

Plump fists rubbed heavy eyelids, then chubby arms reached out towards the uniformed figure of his father. 'Papa,' he gurgled happily.

Marie Louise saw the tears in Napoleon's eyes as he lifted the boy tenderly from his nurse, and the gentleness of his caress on the baby's curls. Sadness struck deep in Marie Louise's heart, not that she was envious of the child's love for his father, but the look of love and pride in Madame de Montesquiou's jealous eyes and the careful manner in which Napoleon returned the baby to her made her realize, for once and for all, that she was as firmly shut out of her son's life as if she had died at the moment of his birth.

Without a word she walked sadly from the room.

CHAPTER 11

PARIS, 1812

THERE was no time for Marie Louise to fret, over either Montebello's disgrace or her baby's alienated love, for almost at once storm-clouds loomed over Paris, shutting out sunshine and casting a menacing gloom over the city's gaiety.

'Tsar Alexander becomes a danger to me,' Napoleon confided to his wife, and Marie Louise felt her heart flutter in agitation. 'Great events are in the air, ma bonne, and soon I must go to put an end to Russia's threat.'

'Then—then you will have to leave me!' she cried involuntarily, and the thought terrified her. With his strength close by her, she had had no need to fear this foreign country, but once he was gone she would be defenceless. Frenchmen had no love for an Austrian empress, and she had not yet learnt their ways in order to charm them.

'You will be safe, ma petite, have no fear.' Napoleon's voice was calm and reassuring, but his next words filled Marie Louise with pleasure.' I shall call a conclave of my allies first in Dresden, your father amongst them. And there I shall confide you to his care for a time. Does that not please you, Louise?'

Marie Louise clapped her hands in delight. 'Oh indeed it does! You are so thoughtful, Napoleon. There is nothing I should like better than to see Papa and assure him yet again of my happiness with you.'

Spring showered its benison of sunshine and warmth on the

great Imperial coach which bore Napoleon and Marie Louise to Dresden, while the infant King of Rome remained in Paris. 'Remember your position as Empress of France,' Napoleon remarked quietly as the coach drew up at the palace. 'Do not throw yourself impetuously upon your parents but remember your dignity at all times.'

Marie Louise felt her heart contract. It was enough to miss Papa so dreadfully, but to have to greet him in icy, regal aloofness was almost more than she could bear.

As soon as she entered the room, magnificently gowned and bejewelled as Napoleon had ordered, she saw her father and joy leapt in her to see the warmth of the smile that came instantly to his face. His young wife, Maria Ludovica, advanced first, her arms outstretched. Marie Louise proffered her hand coolly, and saw the dismay on her stepmother's face.

Then Papa came forward, and Marie Louise could not resist squeezing his hand fervently, her face radiant, and felt irritated by Maria Ludovica's insistent hand which drew her away to sit beside her on the sofa. At once she was all chatter and animation, as though presuming an intimacy between them which had never existed. Marie Louise instantly felt withdrawn. Papa was deep in conversation with Napoleon and she could feel only pleasure that the two men she loved so well seemed to like and respect each other at sight.

'Are you listening to me?' Maria Ludovica questioned sharply, her arm sliding through Marie Louise's.

'Yes, of course.' Then Marie Louise saw that her step-mother's eyes were riveted to something which obviously took her attention. Marie Louise followed her gaze. Opposite the sofa, on the far wall, a long mirror reflected the figures of the two young women, the one dark and attractive and soberly dressed with but a few jewels, while the fair, regal woman was a blaze of jewels and iridescent brocade. The contrast was too marked to go unnoticed. At once Marie Louise felt pity for her stepmother who, she knew, yearned for wealth. No doubt at this moment she was bitterly jealous of Marie Louise's success and happiness. The young Empress felt her dislike thaw at once, and impulsively she leaned over and patted Maria Ludovica's hand affectionately.

'There is much in France which has made me happy, Maria, but I have given up much which I loved too. I miss my family and Austria deeply.'

Maria Ludovica's gaze turned to Napoleon, still deep in conversation with her husband. 'Indeed, perhaps you deserve your wealth,' she commented drily, eyeing Napoleon's short, stocky figure disdainfully. 'It would seem you have more than a hundred attendants in your train, and I but two, but I think I should demand a higher price if I were to render the sacrifice you have done.'

Marie Louise blinked. 'I do not understand you, step-mother. You must know from my letters how happy I am.'

'So you say, my dear, but I know how you hate to hurt your father.'

'It is true, I swear it! See how my husband heaps me with wonderful clothes and jewels and all I ask! How could I not admire and respect a man so generous?'

Maria Ludovica's dark eyes were regarding the oblivious Napoleon with glittering scorn. 'There is no doubt he treats you well, child, but is it worth the disgrace of having to sleep with—that?'

Marie Louise fell back against the cushions of the sofa, the breath driven from her body by the force of the cruel words. Maria Ludovica smiled brilliantly at Napoleon and Francis as they came over to join the ladies.

'If you will excuse me, Madame,' Marie Louise said quietly, 'it is late and I must rejoin our other royal guests.'

With dignity she escaped the embarrassing scene, but late that night she wept bitterly over her stepmother's words. Drying her tears before Napoleon came to bed, Marie Louise tried to hide the hurt but he was quick to sense it.

'Tell me,' he commanded at last.

'My stepmother is jealous of my wealth, that is all. And I fear she does not like you over-much.'

'Is that all? Then I must endeavour to win her over,' Napoleon smiled, confident as always of certain success. 'A little flattery and a few jewels should soon amend the situation, so fret no more, Louise. Come, kiss and forget.'

Thus, amid the pageantry of the days that followed, the banquets and theatre visits, the balls and concerts, Napoleon plied the Austrian Empress with priceless gifts and cajoled her with flattery. Maria Ludovica accepted all gracefully, but to Marie Louise's perceptive eye it was evident she loved the upstart Corsican no better for it. Even her father, she thought, regarded Napoleon with the deferential manner of one who feared and respected rather than one who held in affection an esteemed son-in-law. Only her father's trusted Minister, Metternich, gazed at Napoleon with genuine admiration in his eyes. None looked with love, and Marie Louise felt yet more tenderness towards her husband because of it.

As the end of May drew in sight, Marie Louise's fear mounted. The days were fast slipping by and soon Napoleon would be gone, leading his forces against the might of Russia.

'My husband, I shall be so afraid without you,' she would sob into the warmth of his shoulder in bed.

'In the bosom of your beloved family you will be safe, ma petite. Confide in your father. Continue to win over the

Empress with more gifts and by the time you return to France in a month or two, I shall be already on my way home to you, have no fear.'

But despite the tumultuous applause and adulation that greeted their every appearance, Marie Louise's heart was encircled with pain. At last, at midnight on Friday, Napoleon rose to bid farewell to his guests.

'At three in the morning I go,' he announced curtly. Cheers greeted the news, but Marie Louise felt only numb with despair.

He would not come to bed. Forlornly she watched him supervise the final packing and preparations until at last all was ready. The valet Constant hovered behind, his master's cloak and hat ready in his hands. Marie Louise stood dumb, a lump clogging her throat and her hands raised in appeal. Napoleon cleared his throat abruptly.

'Delay an hour, Constant. Let my men know.'

'But dawn is already breaking, Your Majesty.'

'Nevertheless, do as I say. Begone.'

Marie Louise fell into his arms, tears blinding her. Napoleon led her gently towards the bed.

'Come now, my sweet. You must be brave. One hour more together, and then I must away, but let it be an hour to remember.'

At four o'clock, he rose hastily, and dressed.

'Have courage, ma bonne, and help me for I too am sad and anxious. Let us part quickly, so as not to prolong the sadness.'

A swift kiss and he was gone. Marie Louise fell, sobbing, across the bed, still warm from his body, and gave herself up to unrestrained grief. God grant he would come home safe and unharmed soon!

An hour later she rose, red-eyed and weak, and took pen

and paper. As always when her heart was in turmoil. Marie Louise committed her emotions to paper.

'. . . How miserable and lonely I am without him. I try to reason with myself, but I feel certain that until I see my husband again I shall feel just as desperate as I do now.'

Soon Napoleon's letters began to arrive, many and often, and all promising that the separation would be short. '*Adieu ma douce amie*. . . . I kiss you a thousand times. . . . I wish I was with you. . . . *Tout à toi*. . . . A tender kiss for my Louise. Napoleon.'

His messages, always brief but urgent and impassioned, brought Marie Louise infinite happiness, helping to offset the loneliness and longing which persisted despite her family's attentions. Papa Francis was most solicitous and arranged many functions in Prague to entertain her royally, and named a number of his gentlemen to be officially attached to her suite. Marie Louise was grateful, but of all the gentlemen only one caught her attention momentarily—the fair-haired, handsome soldier with a black patch over his eye.

'Who is the one-eyed General?' she enquired of Maria Ludovica, having decided to ignore her stepmother's taunts about Napoleon. After all Maria Ludovica had hated him for so long, it would be foolish to expect her to come to like him suddenly. In time, perhaps, her attitude would soften.

'Adam Neipperg. He is one of our diplomats and travels widely on Government business, A pleasant fellow and a very amusing conversationalist.'

'How unfortunate he has lost an eye, but the other looks penetrating and lively. He looks interesting.'

Maria Ludovica laughed. 'So many other women have found, my dear, and his present mistress loves him well. But come, help me arrange a grand Ball for your sisters, for there is so much to prepare.'

So for two months Marie Louise stayed with her family, heaping them all generously with gifts and money, and the interesting one-eyed soldier was soon forgotten.

It was a hot July day when Marie Louise was forced at last to bid a tearful farewell to her family and return to Paris, to attempt to lead the French court alone without Napoleon's help. It was just as she was entering her great coach to depart that a messenger came galloping into the palace yard.

'A moment, Luischen,' her father murmured, 'this may be news from Napoleon.'

He broke the seal of the letter the messenger presented and read swiftly, then turned to take Marie Louise's hand. 'The Emperor Napoleon has crossed the Niemen and has entered Russia. Go now in peace, my child, for he fares well.'

After three weeks' journeying Marie Louise reached Paris. The sober little toddler who gazed at her seriously and murmured 'Maman' politely, amazed her; in so short a time he had grown from a babe in arms to a sixteen-months-old child. His alert eyes and grave, intelligent manner delighted her, but once again she felt the pangs of estrangement, of not really knowing the son she had borne.

She bore Napoleon's absence only with difficulty, reading and re-reading his copious letters avidly. 'My affairs are going well. . . . My health is good. . . . Kiss the little King for me. Napoleon.' She sent him a portait of the baby, knowing how the sight of the beloved little face would cheer him, and was gratified later to learn that he had displayed it to his troops, to encourage and inspire them on the eve of a great battle they called Borodino.

Word came that the battle was a success for Napoleon and that he was leading his victorious army on into Russia's snowy wastes, onwards towards Moscow. But soon rumours came that all was not well, that French troops were falling victim to fatigue and the icy weather. Marie Louise, forlorn and fretful at Napoleon's prolonged absence, grew thin and lethargic and could not bring herself to appear publicly.

'But you must, Your Majesty,' Montebello urged, 'or you will lose favour with the people. They look to you for the display of ceremony Napoleon usually gives them.'

'They like me no more than they have ever done,' Marie Louise answered sadly. 'Two years I have been Empress of France, and to them I am still the Austrian intruder.'

'But they can never grow to love you if you remain constantly hidden,' Montebello reasoned with her, but to no avail.

It was nearing Christmas when the rumours of Napoleon's depleting army were confirmed. Marie Louise could not believe it. Napoleon was invincible—he had captured Moscow, had he not? The most brilliant Emperor the world had ever known could not be defeated thus easily—and by mere snow and ice at that. It was unthinkable. No, he would not give in. He would stay, whatever the difficulties, and bring the Russian Tsar to his knees before he would quit. Marie Louise sighed deeply. She had just celebrated her twenty-first birthday without her husband. Christmas festivities at the Court would be shallow and meaningless without his vibrant presence, and Marie Louise sighed again wearily as she gazed at her pallid reflection in the mirror.

'Go, leave me,' she bade her tiring women as the bedtime disrobing ceremony came to an end. With a languid wave she despatched them, ignoring their low curtseys as they withdrew. She picked up the miniature portrait of Napoleon from her dressing table.

'Oh my husband,' she murmured to it lovingly, 'why are you not here to comfort me?'

A sound in the antechamber caused her to glance up sharply. Someone of her retinue still lingered. A man's voice broke the stillness and Marie Louise started. The Emperor had sternly forbidden male intrusion of her apartments. She frowned uncomprehendingly, and leapt in alarm when a woman's scream rang out. Dear God! Was there a would-be assassin within the palace? Marie Louise held her breath in terror, the miniature clutched close to her breast.

Without warning the door crashed open, and a man's dishevelled figure lurched in the doorway. Marie Louise gasped at the sight of the dirty figure, unshaven and unkempt, the soldier's uniform, tattered and mud-spattered, visible under the fur cloak, and a second later she recognized him. There was no mistaking the keen dark eyes, reddened though they were.

'Napoleon!'

She rushed into his arms, oblivious to the filth and wetness, clinging to him in delight.

'Ma bonne Louise,' he croaked, his fingers gently smoothing her hair.

'I thought you still in Russia, Napoleon.'

'I had to return to you. I gave orders I was not to be announced, for I wanted to surprise you.'

She clung, closer to him, delirious with joy. Now Christmas would be real and meaningful after all.

CHAPTER 12

PARIS, 1813

WITHOUT doubt Napoleon was a fiercely passionate lover and in the weeks after his return Marie Louise, after the deprivation of seven months, lost sight of the world outside as she leapt ardently to return his embraces, basking in the rapture of another honeymoon. What need had she to care about the troubles of the world outside, the pressures of politics and the struggles of others to attain power, so long as she had her adoring husband to gaze upon her with such patent love and admiration?

'The boy grows strong and handsome,' Napoleon commented, watching the little King of Rome as he played. Marie Louise felt only pride at the love in his eyes. 'It is well,' he continued soberly, 'for he has a great destiny before him.'

But Marie Louise's contentment was not to last. As the new year, 1813, cast its wintry light on the Tuileries Palace, the survivors from the Russian offensive began to trickle back into the capital, and from the palace windows Marie Louise could see them, mutilated by frostbite, weary, desolate and utterly demoralized. Their bleak faces told a tragic story. She questioned Napoleon.

'It is true, ma bonne, we took and burnt Moscow, but at a cost. Over two hundred thousand of my army never even reached Moscow, and there poor devils are the lucky few who survived. I must conscript more.'

'Then is the fighting not yet done?' she cried in alarm.

He smiled sadly. 'You do not understand, Louise. The threat is greater still now, and I must fight. But before I go, I must ensure that the monarchy is safe.'

Marie Louise stared uncomprehendingly. She knew nothing of politics, nor did she wish to. Husband and son were all she knew and cared for. The one fear in her mind was that Napoleon would again have to leave her, as it now appeared he would.

'While I was away I understand there was a coup, a plot to overthrow the monarchy. A General Malet—you no doubt heard of it?'

Marie Louise nodded. 'Oh yes, they told me of it. But it was nothing—a madman, they said, who tried to take Paris one night in October. But he was caught and imprisoned by the morning. It was nothing, really.'

Napoleon sighed and stretched out in his chair. 'You do not understand, ma petite. It could have been tragic. However, I must ensure that you and the boy are safe when I am absent. To that end I must appoint a Regent to rule in my stead while I am away.'

'Why must you fight, Napoleon?' Marie Louise asked timidly.

Again the weary smile flickered on the grave face. 'Europe arms against me. I can call none my friend.'

'But my father will never desert you! He will back you, I am sure!'

'You think so? Well, we shall see. But to the question of the Regency. Unfortunately our son is not yet two years old, and therefore too young. I have considered my brothers, but Joseph in Spain and Louis in Holland have their problems. I no longer speak to Lucien, and Jerome has troubles enough of his own in Westphalia.'

So all the Bonaparte clan had been considered, Marie Louise reflected. Madame Mère had no doubt had a hand in the debate with Napoleon over the matter. On whom, she wondered, had their choice fallen at last?

No burst of cannon could have startled Marie Louise more than Napoleon's announcement. 'So I have chosen you, *ma bonne* Louise, to act as Regent.'

'Me?' Marie Louise's voice was a strangled gasp. 'But I know nothing of politics—I cannot rule—it is beyond my comprehension! Oh Napoleon! I am conscious of the honour you do me, but I cannot!'

He leaned forward, taking her hands between his. 'I know you are young and inexperienced, but you I can trust. Will you do it for me, Louise?'

She could not refuse the pleading in his voice and the fear that lurked in his mournful eyes. Despite his attention to her lately, she had suspected that problems still perplexed him although she could not guess at their magnitude.

'I shall make terms with the Pope,' he went on thoughtfully. 'To have you crowned by him will ensure your place in my people's minds, so to win him over I shall reinstate the renegade Cardinals. And you, my love. . . .'

'Yes, Napoleon? What can I do?'

'You will write to your father and say pleasant things about me. Tell him how I like and admire him. Thus perhaps he will not join the European bloc which treatens me.'

'Oh, I'm certain he will not! But I shall do as you say nonetheless,' Marie Louise agreed eagerly. Anything, anything she would do to chase away the haunted look from Napoleon's solemn face. Gratifyingly, he smiled.

'I knew I could rely on you. Always you do as I ask.'

'As my father bade me, as my duty, but now it is my pleasure to obey you,' she answered gently.

'That is what I love most in you, *ma chérie*, your utter compliance. Through you I shall achieve victory yet. Come, let us go to bed.'

But he slept restlessly, and in the early hours before dawn Marie Louise was awakened by the sound of soft moans. Napoleon lay naked, stretched across the bed, stirring and groaning as he slept. A bad dream perhaps, she mused, uncertain whether to wake him, for he slept little these days. Sitting up and cupping her chin in her hands she surveyed him lovingly.

He bore the marks of a soldier, she thought with pride. The slight scar on the forehead and another on his chest were honourably gained at the siege of Toulon, long before she had met him and there too he had earned the wound in his right thigh where a deep white scar still glistened. Two scars on his left leg were souvenirs of Ratisbon and Wagram. He had been brief in his account of them, but she remembered with nostalgia how, as a new bride, she had traced lovingly the outline of each scar and questioned him as to how he obtained it. Poor Napoleon. All his life had been a constant battle and even now, at forty-seven, the prospect of yet more fighting stretched ahead of him.

He groaned again and awoke suddenly, clutching his stomach and curling into a ball. Marie Louise was at once all concern.

'What ails you, Napoleon? Are you ill?'

'It is my stomach. It troubles me from time to time, but it will pass. No, don't ring the bell. I shall see Corvisant in the morning.'

'Have you had pain often?'

'Over the months it comes and goes. It was worst while I was in Russia.'

'But you wrote always that you were in good health.'

'I would not wish to trouble you, to worry you over my stomach cramps. But have no fear, it always passes.'

But in the morning he looked grey and haggard still and, insisting that the attack was over, he refused to consult Dr. Corvisant.

March brought with it the infant King of Rome's second birthday. Then, the Pope having refused to acknowledge Marie Louise as Napoleon's wife, the Emperor decided to declare her Regent publicly in the Salle du Conseil at the Elysées Palace. Her voice shook as she read the solemn oath of fidelity to the Constitution to the assembled gathering, but Napoleon's encouraging smile bolstered her, and she was able to assure the assembly confidently that she would devote herself unreservedly to the happiness of France.

'Oh Napoleon! Shall I really be able to deserve your trust in me?' she asked him anxiously after the ceremony. 'How can I make important decisions in your Cabinet when I know so little?'

'You need have no fear. I shall send my commands to you daily, and any decisions will be taken by the Duc de Cambacères, my first counsellor. You, as my Regent, are the figurehead, an Empress of blood royal.'

Reassured, Marie Louise smiled. But the smile faded when, early in April, Napoleon left to recommence his campaign against Russia and Prussia. To fend off her dejection Marie Louise took up her quill pen and wrote prolifically, loving letters to her husband and beseeching missives to her father. Napoleon had not been deluded by Maria Ludovica's apparent charms as she received his many gifts; he knew her longstanding hatred of him and feared her influence on the Emperor Francis. Thus he had asked Marie Louise to write often to her father, assuring him of Napoleon's good will and affection. Dutifully she did so. Surely Papa would never turn

E

traitor on his son-in-law, the husband of his beloved child? His love for her would deter him from joining the European band against Napoleon.

But she was Regent now, a position of trust. It was her task to safeguard France. Obediently she wrote to Papa, often. The message was always the same.

'The Emperor begs me to say many nice things to you. He is very fond of you; not a day passes but he says how much he likes you. . . . The Emperor begs me to assure you of his friendship . . . to remind you that he is fighting for the future of your daughter and your grandson. . . .'

She was nervous when she presided over the Cabinet. Now she, trained all her life to obey, was in a position to command. The responsibility held terror for her, and it was with relief that she heard the Duc de Cambacères give all necessary orders. Word came of Napoleon's victory at Lutzen and Marie Louise breathed more easily. Of course, wherever there was Napoleon there was success. Soon he would return, the all-conquering hero, and all would be well again.

She peeped into the nursery. Little Napoleon, his fair curls tumbling to his shoulders, knelt at his bedside in prayer while Madame de Montesquiou, arms folded and smiling approvingly, stood by and listened.

'That is good, little one, now say the piece for Papa.'

'God bless Papa,' the childish voice lisped, 'and grant he may give peace to the world. Please, Jesus, make the little King of Rome a brave boy. Amen.'

Silently Marie Louise slipped away. It seemed intrusive, to trespass upon the intimacy of 'Maman Quiou' as he called her, and the boy.

A sadness fell upon her. And as the long days of summer dwindled into autumn shreds of suspicion began to fray her composure. Napoelon's affairs were not going well. There was trouble first in Spain where Napoleon's troops were defeated at Vittoria, and then in Italy. Montebello's hitherto veiled dislike of her master was growing more open. The atmosphere in Paris changed suddenly from abandoned gaiety and certainty of victory, to repressed sullenness and apathy.

And then the blow fell. Papa Francis turned traitor, joining the Allies against Napoleon. Marie Louise was sick with shock and horror, too aghast to believe the horrifying truth. The armies clashed, and at first Napoleon was victorious, defeating the Allies at Dresden. Marie Louise could not rejoice. It was a bitter thought, that her husband now crossed swords with her own father.

But then the tide began to turn. Napoleon's army of a hundred and forty thousand men were beaten at Leipzig and sixty thousand men were lost. Marie Louise was informed that the Emperor was on his way home to France.

'Poor Napoleon,' she murmured sadly to Montebello. 'He will be so unhappy, for he is unused to defeat.'

Montebello snorted, but made no comment. Marie Louise fingered her gown, richly-encrusted with jewelled embroidery. 'Montebello, I grow tired of frippery and vanity. It is not fitting to waste time in trivial amusement and magnificent clothes when times are so sad. Send Madame de Luçay to me. I wish her to order some plain gowns for my wardrobe.'

'Very well, Your Majesty.'

But Madame did not approve of Marie Louise's choice of a new gown. 'Plain black velvet would indeed be becoming, Your Majesty, but the Emperor does not favour black.'

Montebello intervened, as she always did if another presumed to influence her mistress. 'May I remind you, Madame de Luçay, that my mistress is the Empress. Do as she bids you. Black will enhance her fair colouring perfectly.'

So it was that evening early in November Marie Louise sat in her new black gown in her boudoir. A sudden clamour in the distance heralded the entry of a messenger.

'Your Majesty, the Emperor has returned!'

Marie Louise flew to greet him, hurling herself into his arms.

'Are you well, ma bonne Louise, and the child?" he asked gruffly. She could not help but notice his grey and haggard look.

'He is well, and I too.'

Napoleon's eyes suddenly darkened. 'But why are you wearing black, Louise? Do you wear widow's weeds?' His voice was curt and cold, and Marie Louise's heart contracted.

'Oh, no!'

'Then go change at once. You know I have a superstitious dread of black. You have always known it. Go, change instantly.'

Marie Louise withdrew meekly. In the doorway she met Maman Quiou, bearing the delighted boy in her arms. She heard the child's eager shriek, and saw the cold fury in Napoleon's eyes change instantly to pure pleasure. With Madame de Luçay's help Marie Louise changed swiftly, returning soon in a gown of white satin. Montesquiou had left, taking the baby with her.

Napoleon's eyebrows rose at the sight of Marie Louise. She crossed the room and took his hands in hers, noting again with concern the lines of fatigue on his face.

'There now, my love, does this gown please you better?'

He drew his hands away from hers and turned to the fireplace. 'White is the colour of mourning,' he commented gruffly. 'And patterned with pearls—the emblem of tears.'

Marie Louise's heart turned icy with fear. Again she had

done the wrong thing. Was Napoleon blaming her for her father's treachery? Oh, surely not! Tears hovered behind her eyelids, searing and shameful. Napoleon, his back towards her, spoke again.

'Forgive me, Louise, I do not mean to hurt. I fear I am tired and saddened. France is in a perilous state, and I fear for the safety of you and the boy, if I should fail.'

Marie Louise went to him, drawing him round to face her. 'But you will not fail, I know it. You were ever strong and invincible, and you shall be again once you have rested and recovered your strength.' Her eyes searched his worn face anxiously, desperate to make amends. Napoleon groaned and sank into a chair.

'What is it, Napoleon? Are you ill?'

She knelt beside him and Napoleon, smiling feebly, patted her hand in reassurance. 'It is the old stomach pain I told you of, but it will pass, as it always does.'

She rose and crossed the room to the bell. He must eat now, for he must be famished after his journey. As she moved, a familiar pain shot through her foot. It had happened often lately. Napoleon, alert as always, raised a quizzical eyebrow.

'You are limping, Louise, What is it?'

'Oh, nothing, a twinge of rheumatism, Corvisant says, or possibly gout, though I doubt it.'

'It could well be, if you eat as heartily as you did,' her husband remarked. Though she tried to disguise the limp as she recrossed the room to join him, Napoleon's gaze rested thoughtfully upon her.

'Does it trouble you often, Louise?'

'No, only now and again.'

He passed a weary hand across his stubbled chin. 'You know, ma bonne, I could almost swear someone is practising a little witchcraft upon us both. You with your pains in your foot and I in my stomach—do you think someone is stabbing pins into effigies of us?'

Alarm swept through Marie Louise. Napoleon, seeing her startled look, leaned forward apologetically.

'I did not mean it, chéri, I was only joking. Do not look so frightened. A man forgets at the battlefront how sensitive are a woman's feelings.'

But shame and horror were sweeping through Marie Louise. His words had suddenly recalled a long-forgotten scene of two children in the Viennese Palace of Schönbrunn, carefully selecting an ugly soldier doll to mutilate with a bodkin. And at the first attempt the bodkin had torn out Napoleon's stomach.

CHAPTER 13

SPRING, 1814

No sooner was the New Year born than the Allies, including the Emperor Francis, crossed the Rhine and began to invade France. Disbelief and horror flooded Marie Louise. Her husband and her father were now mortal enemies; her husband's, her son's and her own safety depended on vanquishing the Allies. She was but a political pawn, her loyalties torn between father and homeland, and husband and adopted country.

Treachery piled upon treachery. Jonchin Murat, Queen Caroline's ambitious husband, turned traitor to Napoleon, joining the allies and the attack upon his brother-in-law.

'If ever the enemy reaches the gates of Paris, there is no longer an Empire. I must leave at once. I must go,' Napoleon stated laconically. But before he did, he summoned the National Guard to the Salle des Maréchaux and there, in impassioned tones, he commended to their care the safety of the Empress and the infant King.

'I shall leave fully reassured and without the least anxiety, knowing that they will be protected by you. After France, all that I hold most precious I entrust to your hands. You will answer for them. You will defend them.'

Resounding cheers re-echoed round the chamber and Napoleon, touched by the spontaneous token of their affection and loyalty, turned to Marie Louise. She could see the glisten of tears in his eyes. Madame de Montesquiou stood nearby with the little King. Napoleon took him tenderly from her and held the child aloft. There was a hoarse, broken note in his voice as he spoke.

'I entrust him to you, gentlemen. Should the enemy approach Paris I entrust him and the Empress to the courage of the National Guard. My wife. . . . My son. . . .'

The eyes of hardy soldiers glistened as brilliantly as Napoleon's own as the outburst of cheering began again. Marie Louise, deeply touched, led her son by the hand from the chamber, while Madame de Montesquiou followed close behind.

All day Napoleon could not bear to be parted from his wife and son. Marie Louise, shrouded in misery, watched through tear-filled eyes as Napoleon sat in his study, the boy on his knee, and sifted through his documents. Every one he tore into pieces and threw on the fire. The whole afternoon passed thus in almost total silence, for neither Napoleon nor Marie Louise could bring themselves to speak of the coming parting.

Only the toddler, unaware of the significance, clutched at the papers his father perused and chuckled as they blazed in the hearth.

The Empress could find no shred of comfort in the scene. If Napoleon returned a conqueror, it would be at the cost of her father's pride, and if he returned beaten, he would never live down the disgrace. Fresh tears scalded her eyelids, and even when Hortense, Josephine and Napoleon's daughter, came to dinner to say farewell to her father, Marie Louise was still too anguished to speak.

'Do not be so sad, ma bonne Louise,' Napoleon murmured across the candle-lit table. 'Trust me. Do not think I have forgotten my profession as a soldier. I shall beat Papa Francis again. Don't cry; I shall be home again soon.'

But despairing grief filled the young Empress as the hour of parting drew near. She accompanied Napoleon to the nursery where he took a last look at their sleeping son, and she saw the tear that fell on the baby's golden head as Napoleon bent over him.

Suddenly and with utter certainty she knew that this parting was to be final, that they would never meet again. Inexplicably she knew, as surely as if her husband lay already dead. Blotched with tears and swollen-eyed, she tried to hide her face from him, unwilling to allow the final glimpse of herself to be an ugly memory for him to carry into battle. Napoleon put a gentle hand under her chin and raised her head.

'Do not fret, ma bonne. Whatever the future holds, I shall return to you, I swear it.'

Sobbing and choked with emotion, Marie Louise flung herself upon him. In a moment, Napoleon detached himself gently.

'Au revoir, chéri. Take care of yourself and the boy.'

And he was gone. Long after his and Constant's footsteps had echoed away down the corridor and the bustle of their departure had died away into the night, Marie Louise sat weeping quietly. It was nearing dawn when, realizing the finality of their parting in its full context at last, she flung herself across the great bed and gave herself up to paroxyms of grief. The bedlinen smelt of Napoleon's virile body. Marie Louise writhed in an agony of bereavement, sobbing until at last she could sob no more.

The Duchess de Montebello came to waken her and found her wide-eyed already, her face tearstained and swollen.

'I shall never see him again.' The voice from the bed was faint and choked, but the eyes stared unseeingly before her.

'Nonsense, Your Majesty.' Montebello's matter-of-fact tones roused Marie Louise from her lethargy.

'I know it, Montebello, I am certain.' The reddened eyes stared at her lady-in-waiting, hope dead and only fear lurking in them. 'I felt a warning presence near me when last we slept, one I have sensed before in my homeland. It was the White Lady, though I did not see her. She comes only to warn of tragedy, Montebello, and I felt her near me. I know now His Majesty will not return.'

Montebello came closer, her shrewd eyes curious. 'Did you tell His Majesty of your premonition?'

'No. He is a superstitious man, and I did not wish to cause him concern. But I know, Montebello. I shall never see my husband again.'

'Come, Madame, I shall prepare your bath for you.'

In the succeeding days when Paris held its breath and prayed for Napoleon's success, hope flickered briefly when he won the first encounter with the Prussians at Brienne. But it was a futile hope. Refugees from all over France began to pour into the capital as one by one the towns fell into Allied hands. At last the secret dread of all Parisians became a reality; the enemy was marching on the capital.

The Cabinet met urgently to debate what was to be done. Marie Louise sat at the head of the table and listened to the earnest talk.

'The Regent and the King of Rome must leave Paris at once,' many voices urged. 'The Emperor bade us see to their safety.'

'Her Majesty's continued presence will encourage the citizens and the Guard to stand and fight,' others argued, led by Talleyrand. 'Moreover, should the Allies enter Paris, Her Majesty's voice might well carry weight with her father, the Emperor of Austria, to treat us leniently. Her flight will put our people to despair.'

Wan, weary faces looked to Marie Louise to take the final decision. Certain as she was of Napoleon's downfall, the matter seemed of little consequence to her.

'I must do as His Majesty commands. I am willing to remain if you wish it, but the choice must be Napoleon's.

It was Joseph, Napoleon's brother, who decided the issue. 'Paris has no fortifications. What can the Guard, a mere forty thousand strong, do against an army three times that number? And our orders from the Emperor are plain. Here are letters from him written within the last three weeks.'

Joseph opened the papers slowly and read aloud from them. 'You must not under any circumstances allow the Empress or the King of Rome to fall into the hands of the enemy. . . . Should Paris be endangered the Empress and her son *must* be removed to safety. . . . If I die, my son reigns and the Empress is Regent. . . . The Allies would like to put an end to everything by leading them as prisoners to Vienna. . . . I would rather have my son at the bottom of the Seine than brought up in Vienna as an Austrian prince. . . .'

Marie Louise sat silent while her Ministers stared at each other. Talleyrand shifted uncomfortably. 'If the Empress and the King of Rome leave Paris, all is lost,' he muttered.

'Nevertheless, His Majesty is emphatic,' Joseph replied, and turning to Marie Louise he added, 'Your Majesty, it is late. In the morning you must leave early for Rambouillet.'

Marie Louise nodded wearily and rose. Outside the door Hortense was waiting. 'What is to be done, Your Majesty?' she asked.

'I am leaving Paris, and I advise you to do the same,' Marie Louise replied.

Hortense hesitated. 'You know that you are losing your crown,' she said reproachfully. Marie Louise turned a saddened gaze upon her.

'What would you have me do, Hortense? I am helpless. It has been decided for me. All my life I have been trained to obey, and I promised Napoleon obedience. If he is to blame anyone his anger shall not fall on me, for I do what he bids me.'

Hortense turned away sharply. Marie Louise returned sadly to her room while her Ministers gave orders for the Court to prepare for the flight. Too tired to undress, Marie Louise flung herself across her bed and dozed fitfully until dawn.

In the cold March dawnlight Marie Louise dressed in a dark brown riding habit and a long travelling cloak, for the journey would be uncomfortable.

'Is my son dressed and ready?' she asked Montebello.

'Montesquiou is bringing him directly.'

He came happily bouncing along the gallery, excited at being wakened and dressed so early. Marie Louise gazed at him lovingly, his bright, curl-framed face alert and eager.

'Are we going to see Papa?' he demanded happily. With a stab of pain Marie Louise looked over his head at Montesquiou, who swiftly came to the rescue.

'Perhaps. First we are going to Rambouillet.'

'And will Papa come there?'

Marie Louise felt panic-stricken. She could not lie to the child, nor could she think of an answer to quieten him. At three years of age he was growing perceptive, and she saw how his eyes flashed from one adult face to the other, sensing in their silence that something was amiss. The great door of the Tuileries stood open, and outside in the Carrousel the child could see the wagons piled high with treasures and their personal possessions. The sight seemed to confirm his intuition. He turned to Montesquiou.

'I am not going to Rambouillet!' the treble voice shrilled. 'I will not leave the Tuileries!'

'Come now, sweetheart,' Montesquiou urged him tenderly. 'Maman Quiou will sit by you in the carriage. It is a lovely ride. Come.'

'No! No! I will not, and you cannot make me! My Papa is away and I am master here. I *will* not go!'

Marie Louise, agitated by his fears, hastened to soothe him with a caress, but Montesquiou intervened. But the more she murmured and soothed, the more the boy screamed and kicked, clinging to the balustrade when strong hands tried to move him forcibly.

'I hate Rambouillet! The Tuileries is my home! Papa will be sad if he returns and I am not here!' he shrieked. Marie Louise saw his tearful face grow redder with anger. 'Leave me alone. I am the King of Rome!' he screamed in fury, but at last, exhausted and sobbing, he was carried out to the waiting coach. He buried his face in Montesquiou's comforting bosom and sobbed.

Marie Louise sat in silence in the coach, waiting for the horses to start. As the whip cracked and the coach turned she looked once more at the great doorway and the foyer within, the building which had been home to her for four years now. She had known peace and love in this home. She had been worshipped and cared for tenderly here by the greatest ruler in the world. Now that life was ended. Scalding tears rolled silently down her cheeks.

Even as Marie Louise's coach rumbled out of Paris

refugees from outlying districts were hurrying into the capital. Afar could be heard the sound of cannon fire, heralding the Russians' menacing advance on the city.

At Rambouillet Marie Louise wanted to stop, for she was tired and the exhausted little King was already asleep.

'It is not safe, so near Paris,' her ministers warned gravely. 'Move on to Chartres at once.' And when a curt note arrived from Joseph bearing the same message, Marie Louise obediently climbed back into the coach. At Chartres messengers came again to her. Paris was still holding out against the Russians, but there was no news from Napoleon. He was believed to be leading his army back towards the capital.

In the morning Montebello told her it was imperative to leave again at once. 'Enemy scouts have been seen in the vicinity. We must leave for Châteaudun en route for Blois.'

Marie Louise was too fatigued and stunned by the swiftness of events to care. 'The wine is drawn,' she murmured fatalistically. 'We must drink it to the end.'

On the fourth night of her journey Marie Louise arrived in Châteaudun. The town lay in darkness, and only one inn, the shabby little Hotel de la Poste, was still lit by a dismal lantern. The patron, disturbed by hoofbeats on the cobblestones, leaned out of an upper window.

'No room, go away,' he shouted, his nightcap bobbing precariously. Obviously he was unaware of his guest's rank. Marie Louise's attendants banged and knocked until the patron at last relented and opened up.

'There is only one room, I fear, and that it not what you are accustomed to,' Montebello reported after inspecting the inn. 'It is dirty and smells vile.'

'No matter. I am too weary to concern myself overmuch,'

Marie Louise replied. But when she found herself in the re-pulsive little room with its louse-ridden bed she found its stench overwhelming.

'Let the boy sleep here—on the floor, not on that foul bed,' she commanded Montesquiou. Then she went below to the kitchen, deciding to sit there by the fire all night.

Without warning, a messenger entered noisily. 'A letter, Your Majesty, from the Emperor.'

Marie Louise took it eagerly, hope leaping in her heart.

'Ma bonne Louise, I came here to defend Paris but it was too late,' the message read. 'The City had been surrendered in the evening. I am assembling my army in the direction of Fontainebleau. My health is good. I suffer at the thought of what you must be enduring. Napoleon.'

She could have cried aloud with joy. What matter if the capital had fallen to the enemy—Napoleon was alive and well! Oblivious to the others crowded about her in the little kitchen, Marie Louise fell to her knees and thanked God for her husband's safety.

Two days later at the prefecture in Blois, Marie Louise celebrated her fourth wedding anniversary. Stricken by lone-liness she wrote to Napoleon at Fontainebleau. 'Mon ami, I cannot live without you. Let me come to you.'

His answer came back, terse and to the point. 'I also want you, but there are so many plans. Let us wait.' No mention of their anniversary, Marie Louise noted sadly. Still, Napoleon had so much on his mind at the moment, it was under-standable.

He had more on his mind than she realized. The Allies were demanding the Emperor's abdication. He wrote urgently to Marie Louise begging her to write at once to her father, reminding him that Marie Louise and her son were his,

Francis', responsibility. 'Remind him of his promises,' Napoleon scrawled.

Obediently Marie Louise wrote and waited anxiously for a reply. A lady of her Court, left behind in Paris earlier, now rejoined the court in Blois. Marie Louise demanded news from her.

'The people have gone over to the enemy, Your Majesty. They hail the return of the Bourbons and await happily the return of Louis XVIII.'

'And His Majesty?'

'They say the Army, under General Marmont, has deserted him. They would force him to abdicate.'

'Never!' Marie Louise cried angrily. 'He will never abdicate!'

But in a bright April morning when sunshine steeped the town in blessed warmth, Colonel Galbois came galloping. His news was unbelievable. The Emperor, in the interests of peace, had renounced all claim to the French throne both for himself and his heirs.

Marie Louise sat stunned. 'Is it really true, Galbois?' He nodded silently. 'Oh, poor Napoleon! Surrounded by traitors! He must be so miserable!'

Suddenly she stood up, for once determined. 'I must go to him, Galbois, I shall return with you to Fontainebleau. Napoleon has need of a friend by his side.'

Galbois shifted uncomfortably. 'I fear it is impossible, Your Majesty. I cannot risk your falling into enemy hands. A letter I will gladly bear him—but not your person, Madame, for the responsibility is too great.'

'You are right, Galbois, and I should not ask it of you. Wait then, for a letter I shall write him.'

Sincerely and with deep affection and understanding she

penned her message to Napoleon, telling him how she wished to join him in his adversity.

'Take it, Galbois, and give His Majesty my love,' Marie Louise said simply when it was sealed. 'Wait—tell me—what will happen to Napoleon now if the worst is to happen?'

Galbois hesitated before answering. 'I understand the Allies plan to send him into exile, Madame. To the island of Elba.'

'Banish him to Elba? Oh no!' Marie Louise cried. It was unthinkable. The great Eagle, exiled to a barren island, would surely pine and die. Pity and sympathy for him gushed to flood her heart. 'I must go with him, wherever he goes. Tell him that, Galbois. But Elba! Oh no, not for Napoleon!'

CHAPTER 14

SUMMER, 1814

NAPOLEON'S brothers Jerome and Joseph were most insistent that Marie Louise should leave Blois and travel further south of the Loire. The Empress, wracked now with further stabs of pain in her hands and feet, felt almost too tired to argue.

'I am like a broken reed, tossed along by the currents of a swollen stream,' she murmured to the Duchess de Montebello. 'Always I bring misfortune wherever I go. All who have had anything to do with me have been stricken, and since my childhood I have constantly been running away from wherever I happened to be, I will not move. I shall await Napoleon's orders.'

Montebello murmured assent. 'In any event we must await your father the Emperor's reply to your letter,' she reminded Marie Louise.

'That is true. I shall not move,' Marie Louise repeated.

But Joseph and Jerome were not to be thwarted. 'His Majesty commanded us to keep you safe from the enemy's hands at all costs. We *must* leave, and immediately,' they argued.

'I will not,' Marie Louise replied with equal firmness.

'Then we must make you,' Jerome countered, and to her amazement he took one arm, and Joseph the other, dragging her towards the door. Frightened, Marie Louise screamed for help. Her Chamberlain and other members of her household came running.

'Let Her Majesty go at once!' the startled Chamberlain

commanded. Sulkily Jerome let her go and Joseph, seeing it was futile, let go of her also. The household and the Guard were undeniably on the Empress's side. Joseph apologized. Jerome went off to sulk.

Suddenly Count Schouvaloff arrived, an envoy of the Tsar, bringing the news that Emperor Francis was at Dijon. Marie Louise and her son, he said, were to be escorted to Orleans. The Empress's heart leapt in hope. Orleans was very close to Fontainebleau; no doubt they planned for her to rejoin her husband there. Eagerly she agreed, and penned a hasty note to Napoleon.

'I am leaving tomorrow morning for Orleans. I shall be with you the next day.'

Even the weary journey when Marie Louise was bewildered by pain and fever was not to be uneventful. Accompanied by Schouvaloff and the Duchess de Montebello she sat in the jolting carriage, grey and drawn and listless. Suddenly wild shouts disturbed the peaceful April air, and the coaches lurched to a halt. Marie Louise started in alarm. Schouvaloff leapt out to investigate. Within moments he returned.

'What is it?' cried Marie Louise. 'Are we being attacked?'

'No, Your Majesty. A few Cossack deserters were trying to loot your treasures, but they have been driven off. All is well now.'

Marie Louise sat trembling. They were welcome to her jewels for all she cared, just so long as she and her son could rejoin Napoleon in safety.

On Easter Sunday Marie Louise attended Mass in Orleans Cathedral. As she left the gloom of the church and came out into the bright sunlight, the little King clutching her hand, the Bishop approached her.

'The Duc de Cadore has just arrived, Your Majesty, bearing a letter from the Emperor your father.'

Marie Louise's heart lifted. A reply from Papa Francis at last—now surely all would be well. He would safeguard her interests at all costs, loving her as he did. She broke the seal eagerly.

As her eye travelled the closely-written lines, her hopes sank.

'I have no bitterness against my son-in-law, only thankfulness for the happiness he has given my daughter. As Emperor I have duties. . . . I have allied myself with other sovereigns and I must accede to their wishes. . . . But I should be grieved to harm my son-in-law.'

No promises. No hope. Francis would not prevent Napoleon's banishment to Elba. Pain, both spiritual and physical, wracked Marie Louise's frame. When it was belatedly announced to her that the Cossack looting of her carriages had in fact been a systematic pillaging by the Provisional Government, that even all her own personal belongings including jewellery, linen and plate had been removed, she no longer cared. What was the indignity of having to borrow knives and forks from the Bishop of Orleans, compared to that which Napoleon now faced?

She was too ill and anguished to feel bitter when members of her own entourage deserted her, rushing back to Paris to join the new régime. Montebello noted her pallor and listlessness and remarked anxiously to Dr. Corvisart.

'It is true, she is far from strong,' he admitted. 'The bouts of fever and rheumatism take their toll of her strength, and now she spits blood. This unsettled life will kill her.'

Montebello pursed her lips defiantly. 'Not if the upstart Emperor is banished,' she stated emphatically. 'Believe me, my friend, once the little man of Fontainebleau has disappeared, she will recover.'

'Will she not follow him to Elba?' Corvisant asked. 'The climate there would be most detrimental to her health.'

'Not if I can help it. I shall refuse to accompany her if she insists.'

'Then we must persuade her, for her health's sake and for her child, to return to Austria. There too she could possibly influence her father,' Corvisant mused.

'Highly unlikely. But it will serve as a good argument nonetheless.'

Their persuasive arguments were further advanced by news from Metternich, informing Marie Louise that the Allies, sitting in solemn conclave in Paris, had decreed that after Napoleon's appointment as sovereign of Elba, Marie Louise was to be granted the Duchies of Parma and Piacenza in Italy, to which her son would eventually succeed. Marie Louise was moved. This was proof of her father's concern for her and his grandson. And once in Parma, Elba would be within reach. . . .

Her father wanted to meet her at Rambouillet. Marie Louise packed and prepared. With luck she could yet improve Napoleon's fortunes with Papa Francis' help. She had barely left Orleans when Napoleon's general Cambronne rode into the town at the head of two battalions to escort her and her son to Napoleon.

She was never told of Napoleon's infinite misery the night he took from his neck the little phial he had worn on a thread ever since his Egyptian campaign. She had seen it often, for he never removed it and he had told her once, laughingly, about its contents, a potion specially prepared for him by the physician Pierre Cabanis.

'It is a very strong poison,' he had said, 'a quick relief from the world's ills if ever I have need of a hasty despatch.'

Lovingly he had chased away her fears, but on that cool

April evening in 1814 when all the world looked black and desolate, he drank the contents and was at once seized with agonizing pain. His attendants found him writhing and retching and crying that he was dying.

'I cannot bear any longer the torments I am undergoing,' he moaned. 'Soon to be escorted from my country by foreigners . . . soon to see my Eagles dragged in the mud. . . . I cannot bear it.'

He squirmed and threshed in exquisite pain, and then vomited violently, again and again. By dawn he was still alive, pale and limp.

'I fear the dose has lost its strength,' he complained feebly to his valet Constant. 'I cannot die.'

At length he fell asleep, fitfully, while Constant watched at his bedside. In the morning Napoleon awoke, feeble still, and looked about him.

'Alas, my friend, I am still here,' be moaned softly. He was never to refer to his suicide attempt again.

Unaware of his misery, Marie Louise drove to Rambouillet, where her father had not yet arrived. Her Imperial Guard was dismissed by Schouvaloff, to be replaced by Cossacks. Realization dawned on Marie Louise.

'We are prisoners,' she said blankly, clutching her son close to her. 'I have been duped.' Schouvaloff hung his head apologetically. Marie Louise, near to tears, began to cough and tasted blood in her mouth.

Dr. Corvisant prepared a *tisane,* but it did little to help the hacking cough. The Empress retired to bed, but feverish dreams where the faces of her husband, her father, her son, Montebello, Metternich and Schouvaloff materialized and faded irrationally, precluded peaceful sleep.

The Emperor Francis was on his way. Marie Louise chose a black gown and pearls to wear, to show her dignity and determination, and sent for Montesquiou to bring her son. The aja duly arrived with a struggling child.

'I don't want to see Papa Francis!' the boy was shouting angrily. 'He is unkind to my Papa!' Marie Louise and Montesquiou both tried to soothe and reassure the child, but when the Emperor's arrival was announced, he still hung back resentfully. Marie Louise, however, rushed to the hall to meet him, and the aja and child followed.

'Papa, oh Papa!' she gasped in relief at the sight of his tall, stern figure and, throwing herself upon him, she embraced and welcomed him almost hysterically. 'And see, here is your grandson,' she added, turning to take the boy from Montesquiou. The Austrian Emperor bent to kiss the child, but the boy drew back and eyed him gravely.

'Then go with Aja to the nursery, sweetheart, for I must talk with Papa Francis,' Marie Louise said softly to smooth over the moment of embarrassment. At once the child marched quickly from the room.

The interview with Francis was not a happy one. Pensively afterwards Marie Louise wrote to Napoleon.

'Father has been very good and affectionate but . . . he will not permit me to join you or to see you. . . . I insisted that it was my duty to follow you, but he told me he wished me to spend two months in Austria with the family, then I should go on to Parma, and eventually I could come on to visit you. I know that my father's decision will kill me. All that I desire is that you should be happy without me. . . . I beg you to give me news of yourself often. . . . My thoughts will be with you always. Let us be courageous. . . . I ask you not to forget me, and to believe that I shall love you always. I am so unhappy. I kiss you and love you with all my heart. Your faithful friend,

Louise.'

Tears blotted the paper as Marie Louise wrote, and when a knock came at the door she brushed them away hastily. A small figure advanced soberly and twined a chubby arm about her neck.

'Mother, I do not like Papa Francis. And I see he has made you cry too. He is a bad man.'

Before Marie Louise could protest that he did not understand, the little King stood back and, looking at her thoughtfully, added, 'Is that why you wear your black dress, Mother? Because he is bad and you are sad?'

Marie Louise shook her head silently and took his hand to lead him to his room. It was strange, she thought, that he echoed his father's words. Did black portend tragedy? If so, she would never wear the gown again, but now it seemed too late to ward off the evil that was to come.

Swiftly events took their course. Marie Louise was obliged to receive the Tsar of Russia and the King of Prussia. By now it was plain that she must agree to the Duchy of Parma. Napoleon's letters still swore undying affection for her and the boy, but in disgrace he was booed and hissed from French soil by citizens who had formerly revered him. His final letters to Marie Louise still showed spirit.

'My courage is high. It could only be lessened by the thought that you no longer cared for me. . . . Kiss my son for me. . . . I hope that your health will be good and that you will be courageous. . . .'

Marie Louise wept bitter tears over his letters for now it was clear that she too was to leave France for ever. As soon as she left French soil she would become thenceforth the Duchess of Parma, erstwhile Empress of France.

'But to me,' muttered Montebello fiercely, 'and to all your French followers you will always be the Empress, do what they will.'

It was early May when Marie Louise and her little son crossed the Rhine, out of France forever, and it was an ironic touch that at the very moment she reached Schaffhausen, where they were to stay the night, Napoleon was disembarking from his ship and setting foot on his new domain of Elba. Bells rang in jubilation for Marie Louise's return to her homeland, but none welcomed Napoleon to his barren island.

At St. Polten, where her family had bidden her a tearful farewell four years ago as she went to embrace her fate with a feared and hated man, her stepmother Maria Ludovica waited to greet her. Marie Louise felt a sudden chill seize her body.

'Montebello, I am afraid. I fear the future!' she cried as the coach clattered in the inn yard.

Her lady-in-waiting regarded her reprovingly. 'Why so, Madame? I could understand it if you were now on your way to Elba, to a miserable life with an impoverished, despised Emperor, but you are destined for happier things. Have courage.'

Mama Ludovica came smiling to Marie Louise's carriage and, entering embraced her warmly. But even to Marie Louise, distraught and exhausted as she was, it was evident the Austrian Empress was ill, for she looked so faded and fragile by the light of the yard lanterns.

By moonrise they were entering the gates of Schönbrunn Palace. Pale and mystical the building rose in the half-light, its shutters closed and no lights gleaming. As if the palace too mourned with her, Marie Louise reflected, her childhood home shared her grief.

CHAPTER 15

SUMMER, 1814

FOR all the profuse summer beauty of Schönbrunn, its lush gardens and luxurious apartments and the attentive adulation lavished upon her by her parents and sisters, Marie Louise could not feel the old childhood sense of homely security in the place. Its haunting peace and beauty, remembered so often in nostalgic reminiscences in Paris, no longer had a soothing effect on her tired soul.

To maintain some effect of normality Marie Louise conducted her way of life in her apartments exactly as if she were still in the Elysées Palace with her French ladies and gentlemen around her until they were taken from her and sent home to France. Montebello was among those to leave. Marie Louise could feel no further sorrow, deeply immersed in grief as she was.

It was ironic, really, that the little Napoleon should immediately make himself at home in his new surroundings, settling happily in his rooms and playing interminably with the valet's son. Within days he was beginning to pick up German words and use them as well as his native French. At least there was some measure of comfort for Marie Louise in her son's adaptability, though he still asked constantly for his Papa.

'Tell me about Elba,' she would ask of her father. 'What is its climate and how many people live there?' Francis answered her questions freely, but was reticent, she noted, when she enquired how far the island lay from the Italian coast.

'I should like to see Napoleon,' she ventured at length. 'To visit him at least.'

'Impossible.' Francis was adamant. Marie Louise wept and pleaded, but in vain. 'Your prime duty is to your son,' Francis reminded her sternly. 'Napoleon himself would concur in that. You must remain here with the boy until the Allies have finally agreed in the peace-treaty to your claim to Parma.'

Repeatedly Marie Louise wrote to Napoleon, assuring him of her intention to join him if possible. But no reply came. Marie Louise began to suspect that their letters were being intercepted. To add to her misery her rheumatic pains began to grow more frequent and severe.

Dr. Corvisart was grave. 'I strongly advise a course at the baths in Aix. Not only would the waters be beneficial, but a change of air and scene also.'

Maria Carolina, ex-Queen of Naples, was now once again in exile in Austria. She was no less emphatic in her views than the doctor.

'I have no time for these upstarts, as you know, grand-daughter, for Napoleon's brother-in-law Murat has stolen my throne. But I do believe strongly in the bonds of marriage and in my view your place is with your husband. Insist on going to Elba to be with him. It is your duty. Take your child and go to him.'

The old Queen, sitting in a shuttered room to avoid the July heat, motioned her grandchild nearer. Marie Louise seated herself on a low stool.

'I fear your family has lost its sense of honour, Luischen. To attempt to deprive a stricken man like Napoleon of his only comfort, is monstrous! Yes, I have suffered at Napoleon's hands, but I pity him nonetheless. It is your right and your duty to go to him. Defy them, or escape, disguised. Marriage is for life, remember.'

Marie Louise was torn with indecision. Should she try to join Napoleon, or go to Aix to improve her health first before attempting any such plan? Her cough was worse now, and the rheumatism unremitting.

Emperor Francis returned from Paris, the negotiation for Napoleon's captivity now completed. Marie Louise asked him tentatively about her visit to Aix.

'Dr. Corvisart says it would do my lungs a world of good. And it would benefit my son also.'

Francis's thoughtful face stiffened. 'That is out of the question, Louise. It is possible you may go, though it would be unwise so near the French frontier, but the boy must remain here.'

And so it was eventually decided. Marie Louise, too bewildered by recent events to argue, agreed to leave little Napoleon in his grandparents' care. She was gratified at least to be allowed to take the cure.

'I shall appoint one of my trusted gentlemen to advise you and act as intermediary during your absence,' Francis promised. But Marie Louise was scarcely listening. Already in her mind's eye she was visualizing the sad scene when her little boy would be tearfully waving farewell, unable to understand the reason for his mother's leaving him. When the time came, she tried hard not to weep in his sight, but she saw the silent tears that glistened in his eyes as he waved.

It was a hot, sultry day when Marie Louise's carriage rumbled into Aix. Someone opened the door and lowered the step and as Marie Louise descended she saw a blond man in the uniform of an Austrian general of the hussars, a patch over his right eye. He stood stiffly to attention and saluted.

'Greetings, Your Grace. I am Count Adam Neipperg, appointed by His Imperial Majesty King Francis to attend you. Here are my credentials.' He proferred a document on which she could see the gold seal of the government.

Memory flickered in Marie Louise's bemused mind. The one perceivable eye, regarding her intently, recalled the earlier occasion she had seen him, in Prague long ago. Maria Ludovica had spoken of this Adam Neipperg, of how women found him captivating. But Marie Louise did not find him captivating now. Instead the thought crossed her mind how Maria Ludovica, blithe and gay then, now resembled a piece of Dresden china, fragile and delicate. She was not well, Marie Louise felt sure.

And the arrogant eye still watching her began to irritate her. His gaze was too searching, too intrusive. Was his mission perhaps to spy on her and report her doings? Angrily Marie Louise brushed the thought aside, declining his arm as she descended from the carriage, and feeling instead a vague kind of nausea at the thought of the empty, eyeless socket beneath the patch.

The carriage had drawn up in a drive fronting a house in the outskirts of Aix. Marie Louise could not refrain from exclaiming with pleasure at the sight of it, fresh and inviting and surrounded by trees.

'Oh, what a delightful house! To whom does it belong, Count Neipperg?'

'To a Monsieur Chevalley, a great lover of art, Your Grace. Queen Hortense lived here for a time.'

His reply was courteous and his manner attentive, but Marie Louise disdained his arm and turned instead to speak to her lady-in-waiting, Madame de Brignole.

'It is without doubt a lovely place, is it not, Brignole? But I wonder what fortune awaits me here.'

Count Neipperg hovered close as if awaiting further commands but Marie Louise continued to ignore him and talk with her lady. She watched the Count curiously nonetheless, at once intrigued and repelled by him. He was of average height, a little younger than Napoleon, perhaps about forty, and his fair hair curled tightly about his broad brow. He was not outrageously handsome, not even especially distinguished in appearance, yet the air of mystery endowed by the patch rendered him interesting nonetheless.

And in a quiet, unobtrusive way Marie Louise discovered he was efficient and considerate as well. Every diversion he could devise for her entertainment he prepared for her, and it was not long before she found that the beneficent effect of the baths and the hot sunshine soothed her pain while Neipperg endeavoured to soothe her mind with amusement. Every morning he came to her room.

'What shall it be today, Madame? An excursion on the lake of Le Bourget would be pleasant.'

'I should enjoy such a trip better, Count, if it were in the company of my husband.'

'To be sure. But in the meantime the summer sun would be warm and pleasing. I trust your rheumatism is improving in this climate.'

'I am indeed feeling better, Count, and I thank you for your concern. Let us ride on horseback today, and tomorrow perhaps we shall sail on the lake.'

'As you wish, Madame.' And imperturbably he carried out her orders precisely. Always he accompanied her, always unobtrusively yet within call. Marie Louise found she could ignore him and he seemed not to mind in the least, yet he was warmly attentive whenever she needed him.

During all the diversions he planned, he never spoke of Napoleon she noted. Marie Louise, hungry for her husband

and child, wondered if the omission was deliberate. Did the Allies expect her to forget her husband if his name were never mentioned? Obtusely she mentioned Napoleon frequently to Neipperg, and wondered when the Count's reaction was always sympathetically polite. He would never speak ill of Napoleon, however hated the ex-Emperor might be. Marie Louise grew exasperated.

'I love my husband, you understand, Neipperg? I intend to join him as soon as I can. I love him still, and intend to follow him however far he may fall.'

'As a good wife should. Your loyalty does you credit, Madame.' The words were spoken in the coolest, calmest tones. Either he did not take her seriously, or his orders were to ignore her protests while preventing her from carrying them out.

It was impossible to guess what went on beneath his placid, inscrutable appearance. Daily Marie Louise found Count Neipperg more and more mysterious and interesting, and daily she thrust the contemplation of him angrily from her mind. Her thoughts should dwell solely on the lonely Napoleon and her son. She tried to focus her thoughts on her husband, no doubt fretfully pacing his tiny kingdom, restless and humbled, anxious for her comfort. But daily the vision of Napoleon's face became harder to conjure up, more faint and fleeting. And it became more difficult still amid the myriad diversions Count Neipperg provided. Gratefully Marie Louise wrote to her father to thank him for his provident choice on her behalf.

'Count Neipperg is full of attention for me, and his way of doing things suits me perfectly.'

It was true. He was a gentleman, refined and courteous, cultured and agreeable. He was an excellent conversationalist and a practised musician—what better company could she have chosen for herself? And daily he planned yet more pleasant surprises for her.

'I have sent to Paris for Talma, the renowned actor, to come and perform for you.'

Marie Louise clapped her hands in delight. The actor had been a great friend in the old days and his acting was pure delight.

Another day Neipperg announced yet another visitor. 'I have sent for Isabey who used to give you painting lessons. He will be here directly.' Yet more pleasure for Marie Louise, who adored his company and looked forward to talking with him about Napoleon.

By evening Count Neipperg would play the piano for her. Marie Louise was enraptured. By candle glow he played, smoothly and dexterously, the lovely Beethoven sonatas which the great composer had written in Vienna under her kinsman the Archduke Rudolph's patronage. There was magic in the haunting music, the candlelight and the expert playing of a captivating man. Marie Louise succumbed gratefully to the soothing influence of the peace he engendered, but guilt still nagged her that she could be thus assuaged while Napoleon suffered alone.

One sultry August evening Neipperg was playing while Marie Louise reclined on a chaise longue watching the curtains at the French windows billowing in the evening breeze. The Count's gaze was dreamy as his fingers caressed the keys. Marie Louise suddenly broke the silence.

'It is August 15th today, Count, and my husband's fête day.'

'Yes, Madame.' His voice was low and equally distant.

'I have written to him, and sent him a lock of my hair in remembrance. I told him I was sad today, for how could I be cheerful when I am obliged to spend this anniversary so sacred to me, far from the two beings who are the dearest to me.'

The Count's rapt expression vanished. He turned from the piano and a dark eye stared at her fixedly. 'You have written to the Emperor, Madame? I was unaware of it.'

'Must you know all I do, Count?'

'My orders from His Imperial Majesty your father are clear. I must guard you well. To do that I must know all you do.'

Marie Louise sat forward and cupped her chin in her hands. 'Tell me, Count Neipperg, are you truly my guardian —or my gaoler and my spy? I grant you have cared for me well of recent weeks, but I would I knew whether I can truly trust you as a friend, or must I regard you as a spy sent here by the Government to watch me?'

She gazed at him levelly. Her innocent stare disarmed him and he looked away before answering. Marie Louise awaited his reply hopefully. Now, as never before, she needed a strong arm to lean upon. Now there was no Napoleon, no Monte-bello, no Papa to decide and guide. This man had a decided air of integrity and command, and it would be wonderful to have his strength to rely upon, if only he were to be trusted.

'Madame, you are direct and honest and I can do no less than equal your frankness,' his sombre voice came out of the gathering dusk. 'I am an Austrian, loyal to the Emperor your father and to his daughter in every way. My mission here was to guard you and to prevent your doing anything—foolish.'

'To prevent my attempting to join Napoleon?'

The dark gaze swung to meet her own. 'My concern is only for your welfare, Madame, and to be truthful I cannot see that your future happiness lies in uniting your lot with that of the fallen Emperor.'

'Then where shall I find happiness, Count, if not in Elba?' The plaintive voice shook with emotion. Neipperg half-rose from the piano stool, then re-seated himself.

'In Parma, perhaps, if one approaches it positively and in hope. Soon you will be Duchess of your own province, living in warmth and sunlight and with the power to do as you please in your own duchy. No guards nor spies will dog your way, and there you can plan the life you wish for yourself and your son.'

A pang shivered Marie Louise's heart at the thought of her little boy, cradling for comfort in Madame Montesquiou's arms. It would indeed be wonderful to mother her own child at last in freedom.

'Do you know Parma, Count?'

'I do, Madame. A wonderful country, bathed in warm sunlight and washed by silver rivers, colourful and beautiful. There your aches would desert you for ever. It is a country very French in atmosphere, prosperous and cultured. I think you would come to love it very quickly.'

'Music, and a theatre, and everything?'

'Everything, Madame. A superb Conservatoire, and an excellent theatre. Education is very advanced in Parma. You would feel yourself among kindred spirits.'

'And you feel I should go there, and not to Elba?'

'Emphatically. Elba would be disastrous for you. In Parma you will have freedom, and the chance to ensure security for your son. Your prime concern must be to concentrate on your son's interests, Madame.'

Marie Louise considered his words. 'You are right, of course. I must think of my son and not only of my own deprivation. But still my conscience tells me I should share my husband's fate.'

No more was said, but when letters at last began to arrive

spasmodically from Napoleon, Marie Louise's conscience was re-awakened.

'Ma bonne Louise, I need you, I want you,' went the content of each letter. 'When may I expect you?'

In her mind's eye she could see him, pacing his rocky kingdom restlessly like a caged tiger, anxious for her coming. Tears scalded her eyes. Duty was a terrible burden, for how could she fly to his side if it meant endangering her son's future? Sorrowfully she wrote to Napoleon telling him of her apprehension. His reaction shocked her.

'Come, or I shall have you forcibly abducted and brought to me. Come at once, or my anger will know no bounds.'

Marie Louise was terrified. To fly nobly to the side of an unfortunate, beloved husband was one matter, but to be threatened and menaced by a frustrated demon was quite another. No one knew better than she the rages of which Napoleon was capable when he was flouted. Indomitable, implacable, he would take his revenge in some way. Fear trembled her body as it had done all those years ago when the Monster marched on Schönbrunn, and in that moment of terror, love for Napoleon died.

CHAPTER 16

AUTUMN, 1814

WHATEVER dying embers of love remained which might have been fanned into life, they were finally quenched when further news came to Marie Louise from Elba. It was as she, on orders from her father, was returning to Vienna from Aix at the end of her cure. She stopped for a time in the Swiss Alps, and it was there that Neipperg came with the news.

'A lady and a little boy have been seen in Elba with Napoleon. Rumour had it that it was you and your son, but we now know it to be Marie Walewska and her child. The boy is so like your own that the mistake was understandable.'

Marie Walewska, Napoleon's true love whom he had renounced in order to marry her. Marie Louise was deeply hurt. He had never truly loved her after all, despite his protestations, if he could send for his Polish amour so swiftly. His marriage to her had been one only of political convenience. She had been but a pawn in his game of power. Humiliation killed the last spark of affection for him, and now she could feel only pity for the fallen hero.

'What shall I do, Count Neipperg?'

'Nothing, Madame. Return to your father and do as he bids you, for he loves you well. Once the Congress has confirmed Parma for you, all will be well.'

Yes, Parma. Now the Duchy began to take on the glowing prospect of a promised land, with peace and freedom for herself and her child. But she needed more. She needed a person of strength to lean upon, and there was still so much love in her heart to lavish. And more. Napoleon, if nothing else, had awakened the woman in her and her body craved the love of a man in return. And if that man could be the pillar of strength she needed, then the world would be complete.

Count Adam Neipperg remained quietly as attentive as ever, devising outings in the mountains which would divert and entertain her. Marie Louise loved the feeling of freedom as she scrambled alone with him among the mountains, for her lady-in-waiting Brignole declined such arduous exercise. One day they rowed across the lake at Lucerne. A huge and beautiful castle drew in sight. Neipperg helped Marie Louise ashore.

'The Castle of the Hapsburgs, Madame. I thought you would like to see the home which cradled Rudolph, your illustrious ancestor and founder of your race.'

Marie Louise breathed deeply in excitement. He knew well how to appeal to her romantic soul, and as they wandered about the ruins he spoke quietly of the ancient hero and his deeds, of his prowess in love and in war. Marie Louise could visualize him, strong and formidable and fascinating as Neipperg himself. Suddenly the Count paused and frowned.

'What is this, sticking from the ground? It looks like the head of a very old lance. Let me see.' He left her side and began prodding with his sword at the protruding piece of rusty metal. Marie Louise sat on a grassy mound and watched. At last he freed it, and brought it reverently to her.

'Here, Madame. It could well have been the lance of the great Rudolph himself. Would you care to have it?' The low tones of his voice stirred her deeply.

'Indeed, Count. I am most grateful to you. I shall keep it as a souvenir of a wonderful day.' She breathed fervently and was gratified to see the faint smile that stirred his usually stern features.

That night dreams of the ancient Hapsburg emperor haunted her, and his face bore a remarkable resemblance to the dour, impressive Austrian general who was her constant companion. As Marie Louise lay awake and pondered over her dream she wondered how such peace and contentment could he hers after so much recent bewilderment and anguish. She was lucky indeed to have a friend who brought such solace and comfort. She must entreat her father to allow the Count to accompany her to Parma when the time came. Such strength and sincerity, such calm serenity contrasted strongly with Napoleon's constant restlessness. Neipperg's calm, reassuring strength would be of great comfort in the days ahead.

In Berne, Neipperg provided yet another entertaining evening for her amusement. The notorious Princess of Wales, the huge, ridiculous Cardine, wife to the Prince Regent of England, was invited to dine with Marie Louise and the Count. She was a strange woman, Marie Louise found, overdressed and over-bejewelled and oddly vulnerable in her garish extravagance, yet remarkably frank and pleasant.

September's lush fruitfulness cloaked the valleys when Neipperg suggested he should take Marie Louise to see the celebrated chapel of William Tell. It was one of those still, hot mornings that promises a sultry day when the small party set out on the trip and as the morning passed the torpor in the air grew heavier.

'How my head aches!' Marie Louise complained at last. 'The air is so heavy, I fear there will be a thunderstorm before long.'

Madame de Brignole agreed. 'I would prefer to climb no higher, Your Grace. Pray let us rest at the inn and seek refreshment.'

Marie Louise glanced enquiringly at Neipperg. 'As you

prefer, Madame, but it would be a pity not to see the Chapel. The air higher will be cooler and more refreshing.'

'True, I should be disappointed not to see it,' Marie Louise concurred. 'You remain if you wish, Brignole, and those who would prefer. The Count and I will climb to the Chapel.' It would be pleasant to have his company alone for a time.

He fell into step beside her, his hand cupping her elbow whenever she needed help and Marie Louise enjoyed the comforting pressure. As they progressed, however, the atmosphere grew more menacing and heavy. The sky yellowed and an eerie gloom descended on the valley. Neipperg glanced up.

'I fear perhaps you were right after all about the thunder, Madame. Would you prefer to return to the others?'

Marie Louise's hopes fell. To have to surrender his pleasant company so soon was disappointing. She smiled shyly.

'I have no wish to rejoin the others, but I must confess I am terrified of thunderstorms. Since I was a little girl I was always frightened of them, hiding under my bedcovers in terror.'

Huge drops of rain began to fall and Neipperg seized her arm suddenly. 'Come, we must take shelter quickly. The chapel is too far; let us go to the barn yonder.'

Even as they ran the rain grew in intensity and Marie Louise's soaked gown was clinging to her figure as they reached the barn and stood gasping breathlessly, within the doorway.

'It cannot last long, then we shall return to the inn and order you a change of clothing,' Neipperg said, surveying her with concern. But Marie Louise cared little for the wet clothes. She was enjoying the closeness, the intimacy of the moment. The Count was staring out into the pouring rain.

'There is a building down there, not far away. I think it could be an inn. We could make for that if the rain lessens for a while,' he was murmuring thoughtfully. Marie Louise stood and gazed at him, full of admiration. So handsome, so regal and aloof, so decisive and strong. What woman would complain of being soaked for the privilege of an hour alone with this man?

But the hour became two and then three and still the rain lashed, so dense that it screened the whole valley from their view. Marie Louise began to shiver. The Count took off his uniform jacket and flung it round her then, picking her up in his arms, he ran out into the blinding rain.

Marie Louise, half-buried in his coat, could see nothing, but she felt the virile muscles as he ran and the pounding of his heart against her breast. She was content. He could take her where he wished. It was wonderful to feel a man's strong arms about her body again, and he was making decisions for her.

He stopped, shouted, a door opened, and he put her down. Faces blinked enquiringly at them in the raftered inn.

'A hot bath and the biggest, most comfortable bed you have, at once,' Neipperg ordered, quietly but firmly. At once feet scuttled and anxious hands spread blankets over her shoulders. A sudden roll and a crash outside signified that the thunder had begun. Instinctively Marie Louise cowered. Through the blanket she felt Neipperg's hand on her arm.

'Have no fear, Madame. We are safe now.'

'I—I do not wish to bath, Count. Let me only go to my bed where I may hide under the bedcovers,' she whispered to him, ashamed to let her fear be known to strangers.

'Show us your best room,' Neipperg commanded, and together they followed the shuffling innkeeper up the ricketty staircase. The old man flung back a door revealing a raftered room, a huge bed with a down quilt and a table with a jug and bowl.

'What is this place, innkeeper?'

The *Soleil d'Or,* mein Herr.'

'Good. Bring us food and wine, and then disturb us no more.'

'Very good,' and the man was gone. Marie Louise stared at Neipperg uncomprehendingly. He led her to the bed.

'Undress and dry yourself, then into bed with you, Madame. Knowing your fear of thunder I shall stay with you.'

'But—what of you, Count Neipperg? You too are soaking.'

For the first time, he smiled. Without a word he divested himself of his clothes and then stood naked, and began to unfasten her gown. Marie Louise trembled, no longer with fear but thrilling to his touch. Within moments, the door locked and bolted, they lay in the vast bed and Marie Louise no longer buried herself in terror under the bedcovers when the great rolls of thunder crashed and reverberated over the roof. The innkeeper's knock and his tray of food went unheeded.

In the morning Marie Louise could barely believe what had happened. Overnight she had become Count Adam's mistress, and the experience was wonderful. She had fallen deeply, intoxicatingly, in love with him. This was something new, something powerful and wonderful, and Marie Louise was enraptured. Her ladies' curious gaze when she and Adam rejoined the party was of no account at all to her. Though Adam had spoken no word of love even at the height of passion, she knew instinctively that he cared for her and the knowledge was bliss.

It was October when the train arrived home in Vienna.

The letters which now arrived from Napoleon she handed, unopened as she was bidden, to her father and felt no pang other than pity for the exile. Fear of him had dissipated in her newfound love for Neipperg. And in the reunion with her son. The boy, though delighted to welcome her back, still asked for his Papa, but Marie Louise was able to divert him with promises of the new country they would go to soon, the beautiful land of Parma.

Adam Neipperg remained close by her side but discreet. Secretly he came to her but publicly he remained as aloof and politely attentive as befitted a member of her suite.

'Tell me Adam, truly, was your mission originally to spy on me?' she asked him once, curled happily in the crook of his elbow.

'I was ordered to guard you, and to make you forget the Emperor Napoleon, beloved.'

'And that you have done, but not the way I expected.'

'Nor I, Luischen.'

'Shall you come with me to Parma?'

'Parma is not yet yours. The Congress has yet to meet and confirm it.'

'But it *will* be mine, and then will you come?'

'If His Majesty your father permits.'

'He will. He always does what he can to please me, and I shall beg him to let you come.'

But Parma was not so easy to obtain for the Spanish Bourbons felt they had a better claim to the Duchy. During the winter Marie Louise grew apprehensive. The Congress was meeting now in Vienna but spent more of its time in wining and dining and celebrating the downfall of Napoleon than in negotiating their business, and Marie Louise began to see the golden vision of Parma receding from her view.

'You should join in the festivities, Madame, for the people

may say you are cold or have become French in your opinions,' Adam urged.

'I care little for public opinion,' Marie Louise replied. 'I concern myself only with what is to become of my son and you and me.'

'I beg you attend some of the celebrations nonetheless, for your own sake. And between them we shall ride and paint as you love to do.'

Marie Louise's tired face lit up. 'Yes, come let us ride out into the country, far away to a farmhouse where we may drink milk and be alone and ourselves for a time. Just as we shall in Parma.'

Life would be so beautiful, she reflected as they galloped free into the hills, if only the future were clear. Her son and her lover, and her own beautiful duchy—what more could a woman wish?

The Emperor Alexander of Russia came to Vienna to join in the celebrations and expressed a wish to call on Marie Louise. She confided her dislike of the idea to Neipperg.

'I have no wish to entertain my husband's conqueror, Adam. I do not think I could bring myself to be civil to him.'

Adam regarded her thoughtfully. 'Do you think that wise, Madame? After all, your claim to Parma is not yet ratified, and the Tsar's contempt for the Spanish Bourbons is well-known. He would espouse your cause—and your son's—if only to flout them and out of his admiration for Napoleon it would be a wise move to enlist his friendship.'

Marie Louise smiled at him admiringly. 'Oh Adam, you are so clever! How much I need you to guide and advise me! You are right, of course. I shall receive the Tsar most graciously.'

Tsar Alexander called, not once but several times to Schönbrunn. Marie Louise was delighted when he agreed most chivalrously to champion her cause. 'You shall reign in Parma, my dear,' he assured her. 'You shall reign if I have to fight all the powers in Europe.'

'Then it is as good as done,' remarked Adam in satisfaction when she told him. 'Talleyrand can back the Spaniards but in vain if the Tsar has decided, for the King of Prussia will inevitably join the Tsar's side.'

It was February, 1815, before the Congress finally announced its decision. The sovereigns gathered in Vienna argued and debated and at length declared that the duchy of Parma belonged to Marie Louise and to her son. After many weeks of anxiety Marie Louise smiled again. Life now would be peaceful and unclouded.

On a fine March morning she walked tranquilly in the gardens of Schönbrunn, breathing in the crisp spring air and marvelling at the green buds with their promise of burgeoning new life. New life, for her and for little Napoleon and for Adam. Life would indeed be blissful. She saw a distant figure hastening across the lawns towards her and, recognizing Adam's erect military figure, she held out her arms in welcome. He approached swiftly, his face stern and the muscles about his mouth rigid.

'What is it, Adam? You look anxious.'

'Metternich has just received a dispatch from the Consulate in Geneva.'

'With what news? Oh Adam, tell me quickly! You look so agitated, what is it?'

Adam gripped her elbow, his one eye staring steadfastly. 'Napoleon—he has escaped from Elba.'

The gardens swam in Marie Louise's suddenly misty sight. Napoleon—free—perhaps back in France—searching for her—oh no! Just as life's problems seemed to be resolving themselves!

'The Emperor your father, the Tsar and the King of Prussia have just been informed. They are debating what to do. Come, my dear, let us return to the palace.'

Gently he led her along the gravel path, but Marie Louise was unaware. The sudden news had numbed her faculties. She could not think, could not take it in. . . . The only emotion she could feel was one of blind terror. If Napoleon was to come for her now, the fury he had threatened would be unleashed on her. She clung to Adam's arm.

'Help me, oh help me, Adam! I am terrified!'

CHAPTER 17

1815

ADAM was the proverbial tower of strength.

'Do not waste time in fear, my love. Better by far to make your position clear, both to Napoleon and to your father. Write a note at once, dissociating yourself from Napoleon's plan to regain power, and I shall carry it to the sovereigns. To fail to do so will make them doubt your loyalty, and Parma might never be yours.'

Marie Louise dried her eyes and tried to stop trembling while she wrote, repudiating allegiance to Napoleon and throwing herself and her son on her father's protection. Adam took the letter to the Emperor.

He was even more solemn than usual on his return.

'What does my father say?' Marie Louise demanded.

'He is content, but he fears for your son's safety. Napoleon is marching on Paris and many flock to his cause. His Majesty your father fears there could be a plot to kidnap the boy and thinks it wiser he should have the child closely guarded in the Hofburg.'

Marie Louise made no demur when the boy from taken from Schönbrunn to the great palace. After all, perhaps it would be wiser. It was a strange coincidence that it was little Napoleon's fourth birthday, and he was at a loss to understand why, as soon as his party was over, Maman Quiou bore him away in a coach to his grandfather's. Marie Louise waved him off calmly.

'The parting will be but a brief one, will it not, Adam, for soon we shall go to Parma and my little Prince of Parma will be restored to me.'

Once the problem of Napoleon was solved, she thought unhappily. The Allies were agreed to meet and crush him, but already he was in Paris and Louis XVIII had fled. Napoleon was the ruler once more.

But the parting, she heard later, was not easy for her son. Trustful and confident so long as Maman Quiou was at his side, he raged and wept and was heartbroken when Palace officials removed her and sent her away from him. French influence such as hers was not to be trusted near the little Austrian prince. She could keep alive the cherished memory of his father and remind him often that he was French by birth. Her departure was abrupt and discreet.

Marie Louise had little time to mourn her son's unhappiness, for a letter arrived from Napoleon. He spoke of his triumphal re-entry into Paris.

'I am idolized here and master of the situation. I only want you, ma bonne Louise, and my son. Come to me. . . . Your devoted Napoleon.'

Marie Louise trembled anew in fear as she read. 'What shall I do, Adam? I will not go. I shall never return to France.'

'Take the letter directly to your father. Tell him you wish to receive no more letters from your husband.'

Obediently Marie Louise did so. She understood Adam's unspoken warning, that to do anything which could be construed as disloyal could mean the loss of Parma despite the Congress's decision. And that was unthinkable. Parma was to be heaven, one day.

'There is one thing you must understand, Adam,' she told the Count solemnly as they walked beneath Schönbrunn's leafy trees in the April sunlight, 'I refute my husband, not because I love you—as I do, wholeheartedly—but because I wish to protect my son's future. I would not wish you, of all people, to think I could betray a husband for a lover.'

He took her hands in his gravely. 'I know—and respect you the more for it, Louise.'

She could not bring herself to say more. She loved the Count deeply, but marriage between them was impossible. Not only was he married, but her Catholic beliefs denied the possibility of her own divorce. Adam could be no more than her lover, yet it was not for him that she refuted Napoleon and the chance to return as Empress of the French but for little Napoleon.

And for herself. France held no appeal for her now, and Napoleon was once again the dreaded Ogre of her childhood. Nothing on earth could rekindle in her the love she had once borne him. Adam Neipperg was her adored one now.

He came to her late one evening. 'Be brave, my sweet, for I have news you will not welcome,' he said softly. Marie Louise raised fearful eyes. 'Murat is endeavouring to raise Italy in Napoleon's favour, and I have been ordered to lead a division to quell him. I leave at once.'

Her fingers flew to her lips. 'Oh Adam! What shall I do without you? Who will advise me?'

'It will not be for long, and in the meantime I shall write often, have no fear.'

'I shall lock myself away in solitude in Schönbrunn until your return. Hasten back, my love, for I am desolate without you.'

Schönbrunn's profuse beauty could not alleviate the pain in Marie Louise's heart when Adam was gone. She walked mournfully through the vast park to the pavilion where memories of him lingered yet, and when evening's chill descended she returned slowly to the palace, the dusky patterns of fading sunlight on its many pillars and cornices wringing her heart with its desolate air. The stone sphinxes guarding the courtyard gate and the cold marble statues on the rippling fountains served only to enhance the atmosphere of stillness and death in Adam's absence. Marie Louise shivered. It was not easy to be brave without Adam's reassuring presence. Visions of Napoleon, cold and wrathful, rose in her mind and she was still afraid

News came that Adam's bedridden wife, Theresa, had died three weeks after his departure. Marie Louise could feel no emotion. Theresa's death made no difference at all to her relationship with Adam. Then came news that Adam was victorious in Italy, and Marie Louise was delighted. Not only Joachim Murat would learn defeat at Adam's hands, but also his unscrupulous, scheming wife Caroline, Napoleon's sister. Marie Louise remembered still the cunning girl's gushing attempt at friendship to the new Empress of France. Was it only five years ago? An eternity seemed to span the difference between the ingenuous little Austrian Archduchess then and the wordlywise and saddened ex-Empress of today.

She walked about the empty nursery where little Napoleon's toys still lay. Curiously she looked into the big old cupboard. Yes, at the very bottom lay the box of soldiers she and Ferdi had picked over so long ago, in preparation for their magic. The mutilated, ugly one no longer lay there. Marie Louise was glad. Despite her fear of Napoleon she had no wish to be reminded of her intense hatred of him then.

'Hate! Hate!' The echo of the childish voices, shrill in terror, seemed to linger yet in the air. Hurriedly Marie Louise left. The old emanation of intense fear and hatred hovered too palpably for comfort. And that fear would never disappear completely until Napoleon had been crushed and made incapable of further threat.

'Louise my dear, you look pale,' her father commented one sunsoaked June morning.

'I did not sleep well, Papa. Perhaps I ate too much at supper,' Marie Louise replied. She did not add that no doubt due to the liberal helping of cheese, her sleep had been fraught with terrifying dreams of Napoleon, of him riding triumphantly into Vienna and bearing her off to Paris with him. If only Adam were here; the horror would be considerably lessened by his comforting presence.

In mid-June Papa relented and allowed her son to come and stay for a time in Schönbrunn. Marie Louise sat on a bench in the park under the trees, watching the child's antics as he played with a ball. The garden was flooded with warmth and colour; rain droplets from a recent shower still glistened on the branches and the air was heavy with the scent of roses. Marie Louise mused how beautiful it would be and how soothing, if only the danger of Napoleon's coming could be averted.

It was almost as if Providence overheard. A valet came running.

'There is news, Madame. Bonaparte has been defeated by the Allies in a great battle at a place named Waterloo.'

Marie Louise caught her breath, her fingers flying to her throat. It was too wonderful, too incredible! But Papa Francis confirmed the news.

'It is true, Luischen. Bonaparte has been well and truly vanquished. He declares he will abdicate in favour of his son.' He stroked the child's fair curls affectionately. 'He would have the child Napoleon II, and you the Regent, my dear.'

'Oh no!' The words slipped out involuntarily. 'I hate France! I will never return to Paris! French people dislike me and I them.' Marie Louise's innate honesty compelled the words, for the prospect sickened her. Ambition to govern France, either for herself or her son, were far from her aim. Parma and peace and Adam were her goals now.

'Wait in patience, daughter, for I think it will not be as Napoleon desires,' Francis comforted.

Nor was it. Within a month the Allied sovereigns entered Paris and reinstated Louis XVIII as King. Napoleonic rule was ended, and Marie Louise could breathe again. Her husband was to be sent to the remote island of St. Helena.

'I hope now we shall have lasting peace,' she commented to her father, 'since the Emperor Napoleon can no longer disturb it. This is the only request I venture on his behalf and the last time I shall concern myself about his fate, since I owe him some gratitude for the calm indifference in which he has allowed me to live instead of making me unhappy.'

'Have you no regret for your lost Empire at all?' her father enquired.

'None.' Her reply was emphatic. 'I have no ambition, Papa.'

'Not for your child either?'

'I would not wish him to have to rule and live amongst such a corrupt and fickle people, even though he wore a crown. Frenchmen cheered and adored Napoleon then Louis Bourbon equally, and again Napoleon during his hundred days' return. They are a base and treacherous people. I would not wish such misery on my child.'

'Then you are happy to sign a document in which you renounce all title to the French throne, both for yourself and your child?'

'Gladly, Papa.'

'Very well. Perhaps you will also agree it were best the boy were educated as an Austrian prince then?'

'Of course.'

Francis was pleased. Marie Louise knew his efforts to replace Madame Montesquiou with other governesses had failed miserably, for the boy had rejected them all. Now he found a tutor, the efficient Herr Dietrichstein and little Napoleon's studies began in earnest. Marie Louise watched the little figure, already a deposed Emperor at the age of four, as he walked soberly away to the study alongside the elongated, thin-featured tutor, and she hoped the two would grow to like and respect each other. The boy needed a father-figure now with Napoleon gone and Adam still absent in Italy.

Adam. Pain contracted Marie Louise's heart at the thought of him, lithe and loving and strong. Why was he gone so long? After all these months, with Murat defeated and forced to flee before Napoleon's defeat, why was Adam still in Italy? His letters had been few but very kindly in their gaiety and reassurance, but for the last two weeks there had been no word at all.

Anxiously she enquired of her father. 'I hear no word from General Neipperg. I am concerned for him, for he is invaluable to me. Are you certain he is well, Papa? He could be ill or wounded—or even killed?' But despite Francis's reassurances that all was well, Marie Louise could not resist scanning the daily bulletins from Italy which contained the casualty lists. Daily she sighed with relief that his name did not appear.

She had known she loved him with all her heart when he went away in April; now, in August, his absence had endeared him yet more deeply to her. And now he was a widower, and she an exile's wife. Now they were both free to find happiness together in Parma, even if it lacked the blessing of wedlock.

'Oh Adam! Where are you? Why do you not come to me?'

she wept silently into her pillow by night. 'Come swiftly, my love, for I need you.'

In the meantime, she decided, she could best work for her own and Adam's interests by securing Francis's permission for the General to accompany her to Parma when the time came.

'He would be of great use to me in my household, Papa. I have confidence in him, and I am certain he would give up his diplomatic career if you would permit him, to become Governor of my Household.'

Francis considered the idea amiably enough. 'If you have so much faith in the man, Luischen, then if Metternich concurs, he shall go with you,' he agreed at last, and Marie Louise was delighted. Papa did not suspect the truth of her motives or of her feelings for Adam, but his promise was given. Adam *would* go to Parma with her and her son, and that was enough for now.

'But there is one other matter yet to discuss before you go to Parma,' Francis added slowly as Marie Louise was about to leave the room. She turned in the doorway. There was a reluctant note in her father's voice, as though he were unwilling to speak of it.

'What is it, Papa?'

'Your son.'

'Napoleon? What of him?'

Francis sighed. 'His very name is unfortunate for him. You would be wise to discard Napoleon and call him by his second name. Francis.'

'Is that all? Then that is easily done, Papa.'

'No, wait, child. There is more.' Francis sat wearily in a chair and drew a deep breath before continuing. 'The Sovereigns have debated long about the boy, and in the end they have resolved it would be unwise for him to leave Vienna's safety. You are so innocent and incapable of devious thinking, Louise, that you do not realize the danger of his going to Parma.'

'Not go to Parma?' Marie Louise's voice was weak in surprise. 'But Papa—you promised we could!'

'We feel he could be used by Bonapartist plotters, and you could not protect him. It would be safer—for him—to remain here for a time at least. But there is no need for you to delay your departure. The Duchy is yours. Go when you will.'

'But without my son?' Disbelief and shock made her words almost inaudible.

'Think on it, Luischen. It would be safer and wiser for you both.'

Grief choked Marie Louise. She could make no answer, but simply left the Emperor and returned to her room where she lay across the bed and wept. It was so cruel. Just as it seemed that the Promised Land of Parma and happiness lay within her reach at last, Fate stepped in again to wrench her child from her. Was there never to be peace and contentment in her life?

'Oh Adam, Adam! Come to me and help me,' she sobbed. 'Help me solve the dilemma of how to keep both Parma and you and my son.'

But the weeks passed and Adam did not come.

CHAPTER 18

1816

To fill the great void Marie Louise went on holiday for a time in Baden. On her return to Schönbrunn the lovely old palace seemed chill and deserted with no childish laughter to echo along its corridors. The emptiness was unbearable. Marie Louise drove frequently to the Hofburg Palace in the evenings, to allay the silence amid the chatter and liveliness of her family.

December frosts were nipping the Viennese air when her twenty-fourth birthday arrived.

'I have arranged a grand concert for you, Luischen,' her father told her. 'The Empress, however, does not feel well and will not be able to attend. She sends you her felicitations nonetheless.'

Marie Louise had observed her stepmother's increasing lassitude and pallor. Maria Ludovica, barely five years her senior, seemed an old woman already with her unsteady gait and feeble smile. She was desperately ill, and she knew it.

'I do not mind,' she would comment weakly. 'I have lived to see Napoleon Bonaparte return for his Hundred Days, only to be trapped and shackled. I have hated him long, and it gives me joy to see the Monster brought low at last.

The concert was not enough to lighten Marie Louise's depression. Any event seemed hollow when it was unshared with a loved one. It was during the interval when the door to the Imperial box was suddenly flung wide, and a dusty, dishevelled figure in uniform came forward to bow deeply. Marie Louise saw the man's eye-patch, and her heart lurched.

It was Adam, just this moment arrived in Vienna. He made apology for his appearance to the Emperor, and then turned to Marie Louise.

'I have galloped from Venice without pause save to change horses, for I wished to be here in time to offer my humble and devoted wishes to you, Madame, on the occasion of your birthday.'

The vibrant ring of his voice, remembered so often in the still hours of the night, made Marie Louise tremble in happiness. He had not forgotten her after all. Timidly she offered her hand, and the Count bent low to kiss her fingertips.

'Thank you, Count Neipperg.' It was such a paltry reply to his magnificent gesture, but how, here, could she express her true delight at his return? Longing to be alone with him, Marie Louise made an excuse of a headache and retired with the Count in attendance.

Alone at last she regarded him fondly. He was tanned and weather-beaten but otherwise bore no sign of having changed.

'Are you well, Adam?'

'Perfectly, Louise. And you too?'

The return of rheumatic pains seemed very unimportant now, so Marie Louise did not refer to them. Instead she gazed wistfully at him, revelling in his strength.

'I have missed you sorely, Adam. I have needed you.'

'And now I am here, so there is no longer cause to fret. I shall not leave you again if I can help it.'

He made no mention of Theresa's death. Suddenly Marie Louise realized he would not yet know he was to accompany her officially to Parma. She watched the slow smile grow on his face as she told him.

'But there is one disappointment, Adam. The Sovereigns will not permit my son to accompany us to Parma. They think it is safer for him to stay here—for a time at least.'

Adam rubbed his chin reflectively. 'Indeed, it would be wiser. There is much hostility towards the Bonapartes in Italy and I fear he would not be well received. The Eagle is yet too fresh in Italian memory for the Eaglet to be welcomed. Leave him here for now, Louise, as your father advises. Later, perhaps, we may send for him.'

Dubiously Marie Louise sat down beside him. Her richly-jewelled gown made an odd contrast with his dust-specked uniform. 'I did not expect you to say that, Adam, but if you are convinced it is for the best. . . .'

'I am, my dear, believe me. He has good tutors here and is only just growing to know and love his Austrian relatives. Another journey to a strange land so swiftly would be very unsettling for him.'

Marie Louise nodded, the lump constricting her throat making speech difficult. Adam's arms glided gently about her.

'Do not fret, Louise. We shall be together, you and I, and soon the boy may be able to join us. There will be bliss for us in Parma's sunlight, far from the ice and fog of Vienna. Be optimistic, my sweet. Ahead of us lies great happiness together.'

'You are right, I know it. Oh Adam! How glad I am you are back!'

His shoulder was so strong and fatherly to lean upon, and his kisses so tender and reassuring. All would be well now. How could it be otherwise? Marie Louise leaned gratefully upon him and smiled. Already the fear and tension and anxiety were beginning to slip away. With Adam beside her there would be no more anxiety, no more responsibility and decisions to take, for he would shoulder them all. Marie Louise began to feel more resigned to the idea of leaving little Napoleon behind. It would only be for a little while.

Spring buds were sprouting on skeletal trees when at last Marie Louise was ready to set off on her journey. Vienna was still cold and misty and she reflected how glad she would be if only her son were to come with her. But for him she would have no regret at leaving Austria for a new life. The night before she left she took a pen and wrote to Madame Montebello.

'I leave for Parma tomorrow. I am ill with fever, but it is as much in my heart as in my body. God knows whether I shall have the strength to sustain the long journey in this rigorous season, but I feel sure God will help me. . . . In my grief He has accorded me a great consolation, for I leave my son in good hands and I have the blessing of having a trusted and true friend near me.'

The morning of departure dawned bleak and cold. The boy stood in the vestibule of the Hofburg, his eyes registering dully the piled valises and scurrying valets. Marie Louise knelt and took him in her arms.

'Be good, my son. I shall pray for you, and soon you shall be with me again.' Tears misted her eyes and she could hear the catch in her voice. The boy drew back.

'Do not go away from me, Maman.'

Marie Louise reached for his hand, but he hid it behind his back. 'I must, my love, but we shall not be apart for long. Grandpapa will love you and care for you.'

Dimly she was aware of Adam's presence behind her.

'Do not go away from me,' the child repeated stolidly. She could see the unshed tears glistening in his eyes, and remorse gripped her. She turned an agonized look to Adam, who shook his head mutely.

'Do not go away from me.' Little Napoleon's voice rose to a near shriek. His tutor, Herr Dietrichstein, stepped forward to grip the boy's shoulder. Little Napoleon looked up at him and a strange calm seemed to come over him. He glanced once more at Marie Louise and, seeing she was not going to reply, he turned again to his tutor. 'Come, monsieur, let us continue our studies,' he said in a strained, tight little voice. In silence the man followed the boy from the hall.

A sob escaped Marie Louise and she made to follow him. Adam's hand restrained her.

'Napoleon! Oh, let me go to him!' she wept, gripping Adam's fingers.

'No, Madame. It is over. It is best you go quickly, for to stay will only keep the wound open. Come.' Firmly he led her to the waiting carriage. On the step she paused.

'You are right, as always, Adam. It is my duty to go ahead and prepare the way, so that my son will be accepted as Prince of Parma. I thank God you will always be there to guide my steps, for I would err sadly but for you.'

He smiled as he helped her enter then, as was his right as her Chamberlain, he climbed in and sat beside her. Neither the Emperor nor the Empress were there to wave farewell, for they had been travelling when Maria Ludovica had once again been taken ill. Perhaps, suggested Marie Louise, Adam and she could visit them in Verona on their way, for Maria Ludovica lay abed there.

'Certainly,' Adam agreed, 'but a few days in Venice first will restore the colour to your cheeks.'

In the bliss of Venetian solitude Marie Louise's pain faded. Away from prying Court eyes at last Adam was free to take her in his arms and become once again the ardent lover he had been. Marie Louise was dazed with happiness. Drifting in a gondola with his arms about her, the vexations of the world outside disappeared like a transient dream. The gondolier sang and Adam breathed a sigh of pure contentment.

'Are you happy, Louise?'

'Utterly.'

'And I shall endeavour to keep it always thus.'

They travelled on to Verona. The Emperor Francis was distracted, fretting that Maria Ludovica seemed to become more ill as each day passed. Marie Louise turned from Adam's arms and devoted herself instead to nursing her stepmother, but within days the Empress was dead.

It was mid-April before Marie Louise and Adam reached Parma, a bright sunlit afternoon, and Marie Louise was entranced by the first glimpse of her new capital. Triumphal arches lined the route of their procession and bells clanged out a sonorous welcome. Today she felt well and happy, conscious too that she looked impressive and magnificent to her new subjects' curious eyes for she wore her finest gown and her most superb jewels. Adam's eye twinkled as he sat opposite in the coach, he also resplendent in his beribboned uniform and gold braid.

We shall go first to the Cathedral to give thanks,' Adam told her, and when the bishops and clergy met them from the coach and led them to a dais in the Cathedral, she could barely believe she was here at last. The incense floating in her nostrils, Adam kneeling beside her, the great cupola rising above her and the magnificent Correggio paintings all about her held a strange air of unreality. After the chant of the Te Deum they rode out again along the crowded streets where people waved and smiled and shouted, the pealing of bells and roaring of gun-salutes vying with their cheers.

'Your people pay you homage, Madame,' Adam murmured, his hand covering hers, as they watched multi-coloured fireworks blazing an iridescent trail across the sky. Already it seems they love and welcome you.'

'Yes,' Marie Louise said faintly, 'it is strange but I feel at home here. We shall be happy, Adam, you and I, shall we not?'

'Undoubtedly.'

As spring burgeoned into sultry summer their happiness together blossomed also. The only cloud on Marie Louise's summer-sky was the absence of her son.

'If only he were here,' she would sigh often. Adam took her to task.

'Don't waste time in wishing, Louise. If he is to come, he will. If it is best not, then he will not. But meantime we have work to do here, and we should bend our minds to the task.'

'But I miss a child's warmth and sweetness.' Her voice was plaintive. Adam smiled indulgently.

'There may be other children yet to come.'

'Dr. Dubois said I should never bear another child after such a confinement.'

It seemed to matter little, somehow, in the peace and leisurely pace of life in Parma. Day by day Adam seemed to grow more and more popular with the people and it was not surprising, she reflected contentedly. He was so clever and perceptive, so capable and responsible and at the same time so concerned for his new country's welfare. He worked hard, lifting all the burden from her weary shoulders. Life became dreamily comfortable and peaceful for her, and her love for Adam grew.

'I want only to shield you,' he remarked when she attempted to express her gratitude for all he had brought into her life.

'Shield me? From what, Adam?'

'From worry, from fear. From all the anxiety that accompanied your former way of life.'

He never mentioned Napoleon and Marie Louise was thankful. The Eagle, his eyrie now restricted to a rocky island far away, rarely entered her thoughts nowadays and whenever he did it caused a sudden shudder. Not revulsion, she realized, but fear still flickered at the memory of the terror he could once arouse in all from paupers to Princesses.

It was the sultry heat of September, she decided, which caused her to feel so queasy, or maybe a surfeit of roast duck. When the physician, his examination concluded, confided his diagnosis, Marie Louise was startled.

'Pregnant? Are you sure, doctor?'

It was unbelievable, but as certainty grew Marie Louise was overjoyed. She could not wait to break the news to Adam. He was working in his study but he put down his pen at once when she entered, his face creasing into a warm smile.

'Adam, I am so happy!' Marie Louise cried, clasping her hands in happiness. His smile widened.

'And what is it that gives you such pleasure, my sweet? A new bird or pet rabbit perhaps?'

'No, beloved. A new creature, however. I am to bear your child, Adam.'

She saw the look of perplexity which quickly gave place to a yet more radiant smile. 'Are you certain? It would be so wonderful. But are you not anxious about public comment?'

He was referring to their illegal union, incapable of legalization while Napoleon lived. Marie Louise shook her head firmly.

'No, Adam my love. I fear nothing while I have you. You —and my children—are all I wish for in this world, and crown and sceptres are as nothing beside my treasures. This child will be mine to keep and love.'

'Are you happy then as we are, beloved? Would you go back and change anything that has happened?'

'Now that I have you, my world is perfect. I would change nothing.'

He took her in his arms and she cradled adoringly into the warm strength of his embrace. It was true. She had renounced an Imperial Crown and even, so it seemed, the company of her son temporarily, for the love of a fine man, but she would forego much more to be certain of his love throughout her life. The elegance of France, the splendour of the Austrian court—all was well lost for the blessing of the simple, love-filled life which lay soothingly around her now in Parma. Marie Louise was content.

EPILOGUE

MARIE LOUISE bore Adam a daughter and, four years later, a son. Her first child, Napoleon's son, she never saw again except on brief visits to Vienna, and when he died of consumption at the age of twenty-one she was stricken with remorse on account of her neglect of him, however it might have been forced upon her.

Her happiness with Adam Neipperg lasted until his death in 1829. Their's was a morganatic marriage, not legalized even after Napoleon's death from cancer of the stomach in 1821, three months before her son was born.

Heartbroken after the deaths of Neipperg and of her first-born son, Marie Louise grew rapidly older and more infirm. At the age of forty-three she made a secret marriage of convenience with the Count Charles de Bombelles, a month before her father's death. Bombelles was another man of strength, a father-figure for her to lean upon in her task of governing the Duchy of Parma.

Marie Louise was a stoic figure, working hard in the hospitals during the cholera epidemic of 1836 despite her fragile health. In 1847 she was ill in bed on her fifty-sixth birthday, and five days later she died of rheumatic pleurisy.

All quotations from her letters in the text are authentic.